No Strir

Kindle Edition

First Edition

This is a work of fiction. Names, character, places and incidents are either the product of the author's imagination or are used fictitiously, and any resemblance to actual persons, living or dead, business establishments, events or locales is entirely coincidental.

Find out more about the author and upcoming books online atwww.hilarystormwrites.com

Paperback Cover Design by Bookfabulous Designs

Editing by Tiffany Tillman

Photograpy by Furiousfotog

Printed in the United States of America

Dedication

To those who aren't afraid to fight for their dreams, no matter how high the reach.

Make It Happen

~Hil

Prologue

Luke

Life can change in a heartbeat. Everything you know can become a memory, and the future can be left in the hands of something greater than you can control.

I work hard to remain a free spirit with no intention of *ever* being tied down. My life is a whirlwind, and I don't have time for commitments that I can't promise to keep.

I live for the now and don't worry about what could be or what should've been. This is my life.

I'm the guitarist for the band 'Rebel Walking'. I love what I do and would never do anything to destroy that. That is, until *she* came crashing through my world.

Lilly is the feisty bass guitarist that has been fucking with my head for a few weeks. Her teasing has almost brought me to my knees, but I've managed to refrain from going there. Her efforts have increased over the past few days, and I'm about to say *fuck it* to all of the consequences that may come from my actions.

The days of us chilling together innocently are about over because I have a feeling that once I get my hands on her, we'll never be the same.

Chapter One

Luke

Shit, how am I supposed to walk away from her? I just want a little taste. Except she is forbidden and I'm not supposed to cross that line. That's just a recipe for disaster and almost a promise of what's destined to come.

She licks her lips and looks at me through her sultry eyes, all but demanding me to touch her. My attention follows her hand as she runs her finger across her lips, dragging the bottom one slightly as she begins to move her hips with the beat. *Shit, I can't take it anymore.* Her fingers run over her chest and I notice the hardness of her tits pressing through her shirt. She focuses on each nipple, knowing that she's torturing me, circling each one and watching my face for a reaction that I'm holding back on purpose. *How far will she take this?*

I give her a small smile when her hand moves further south. My eyes move with her fingers, and I'm pretty sure my lungs are not moving the entire time she unbuttons her jeans. A moan escapes my throat when her hand disappears inside the zipper. She lays her head back against the wall and spreads her legs a little wider and continues along the path of my destruction.

I lean back against the wall behind me and brace myself for what she may throw in my direction. She is fucking sexy as hell right now and there is *no way* that I'm walking away from her tonight. I'll face the Walker brothers another day. *Fuck them!*

They should see her right now. I don't have to answer to them anyway.

Her hand moves even lower and I look up to watch her face. She is relentless. The look in her eyes almost has me moving the five feet across the small hall to help her get exactly what she's asking for. Her right hand slides up her shirt, showing off some of her ink as she starts to rub and pinch those gorgeous fucking tits again. Her shirt is in the way, but my mind has no problem imagining how hot they really are.

The ultimate test on my resolve is when she pulls her bra down and I see her nipple through her shirt. I can tell for the first time she has her nipples pierced, and damn I want to run my tongue over each of them. She pulls on her piercing just enough to get that little bit she needs to go over the edge. Fuck, I don't think I've *ever* seen a girl look this sexy during an orgasm. She doesn't shy away from her moans and groans at all, and her ruthless behavior has my dick so hard that I can't take another second of this torture. I move forward and watch her eyes as I approach. She smirks and pulls her bottom lip between her teeth. Our bodies collide and the rush of being in the moment overtakes me. Her tongue piercing bumps against my tongue and my thoughts instantly think of how that would feel on my dick.

She puts her tongue deep into my mouth and manages to lick her way around my mouth and lips. *Damn, she's aggressive and I fucking love it!* This is *not* the same girl that everyone else sees. What happened to 'sweet' Lilly?

I push her back against the wall and start to move her shirt up right as I hear Taron's voice just around the corner. Lilly grips my t-shirt with both hands and pulls me through a door. I don't have time to care about where we are. It's a dark room and for all I know it's a damn bathroom. Our hands pull and rip at the material separating the heat of our bodies. She matches my desperation and we fight for the connection of naked skin against skin.

She isn't holding back at all. One of her hands is pulling at my belt buckle and the other is gripping me through the denim. Damn, she's trying to run this show and I'm not having that. I flip her around to face away from me and pull her body flush against mine. Her heavy breathing is echoing through the room.

She begins to roll her head around my chest and then she suddenly stops everything. Her heavy breathing stops, her body tenses up, and her hands quit exploring my body.

"Did you change your mind?" My voice comes out even deeper than normal when I whisper in her ear.

Lilly

I've wanted this for so long and he is *still* pushing me away. What exactly does a girl have to do to get him to notice? I thought we were finally on the same page and then he pulls back just as I finally get my hands full of him. I'm so tired of his rejection. *Fuck this.*

His voice moves through my body. I can't help but close my eyes and enjoy the closeness for as long as it lasts. My fingers still tingle from the grip I had on his bulge. I know I felt metal beneath that denim and I *definitely* plan to explore that in detail before this is over. *Change my mind? Not on your life, buddy.*

I use what's left of my determination and slide my right hand behind me. My entire hand is filled with this man's dick and it should scare me. The anticipation has me holding my breath for him to touch me, whisper against me, kiss me, lick me, nibble on me, bite me, or just do *anything* before I lose it. I squeeze my hand around him and begin rubbing the full length of his bulge. The first sound from him is a moan, or would you call it a groan? Whatever it is, it's deep and sexy, and I want to hear it more.

He finally begins to move with me and I feel his fingers brush across my nipple as he ends with a flick before he moves to the other one. Holy shit, I've never had these sensations flow through me before. I need him to touch me and he isn't disappointing when I feel his hand slide down and into my jeans.

His finger finds my newest piercing and my knees almost buckle with the sensation that explodes through my core. Now it's *my* breathy moan that can be heard. Here we are, me standing with my back against him, no space separating our bodies. He has managed to reach around and torment my piercings in record time and I *still* have a denim barrier between my hand and his piercings.

He begins to move his fingers and all of my thoughts become jumbled as I lose any care about seeing his metal for the moment. This feeling is about to send me through the roof. Thank god I got this piercing, but not having sex for eight weeks has left me *very* ready to get some relief. He works me until I'm on the verge of screaming his name, managing to pull near painful sounding moans from my mouth. His strong arms hold me up, and I'm positive that I'd fall to the ground if he wasn't holding on to me.

"Shit, Lilly. You're so fucking hot, you're killing me here." His whisper gives me chills and I move to turn and face him. He's taller than I am, so I have to reach to wrap my arms around his neck. My body naturally wants to climb onto him, latch on, and never let go—hold on for the ride of my life, but I fight the urge to climb.

"Luke, I want this. Please don't stop." I sound so weak and pathetic, but I need this. I'm tired of fighting this attraction. All of those days of relentless flirting and back and forth comments have been torture on me. He *has* to want me just as bad as I do him.

"Oh, I'm not stopping. This is happening. You will feel every inch of me, filling you up so much that you won't know whether to scream or quit breathing all together." His face is lined up with mine, and I can feel his intense stare even though it's dark. The intensity has my heart racing so fast and I can hardly breathe as I wait for him to do something.

He moves his hands to lower my jeans. I let him pull them completely off of me. *When did I become this helpless mass of melted flesh? What is happening?* I wait for him to move and *damn* does he move in all the right ways. He runs his lips up my leg all the way until his mouth is stopped right on the edge of my panties. I listen to his heavy breathing and wait again for him to move. My expectations of him being fast and furious have me confused every time he pauses.

I run my fingers through his hair in hopes of encouraging him to continue. He hooks his fingers on each side of my panties and begins to slide them slowly down my legs. The light brush of his fingers sends chills rushing through my body.

His tongue is the next thing I feel when he runs it over my slit. In an instant, he forces his shoulders between my legs and begins to lift me up higher on the wall. I brace my palms flat against the wall near my hips and notice the scrape of the wall on my back as he continues to raise me. He fills his hands with my ass and pulls me in to devour the juices he has already created.

He nibbles and licks his way straight to my sweet spot and has me panting and moaning again in no time. I fight the urge to scream when he brings me over the edge, straight into the best orgasm of my life. The way he sucks on my piercing, pulling on it just slightly, leaves me undone and whimpering without comprehension of anything else in the world.

"You taste so fucking good. I could do this every day." His deep grumble is extremely sexy and pulls me back to the reality that I'm about to finally get what I've been waiting for. With a sway of my hips, I start to feel him working his pants open and hear the sound of him tearing into the condom with the same sense of urgency that I feel.

He guides my legs off of his shoulders and I fall perfectly to the position where he's at my entrance. I feel his thickness and can tell this is going to be as fantastic as I've imagined. He places his hands on the wall on each side of my face and leans in close. His tongue invades my mouth and I can taste myself on him. I accept his roughness and match him with each brush of his tongue. His kiss is passionate and hungry, just like I am right now.

My head falls back against the wall and he moves his hands to my breasts. He focuses on my nipples and the jewelry, making his touch almost unbearable. My moans begin again and I wonder if I'll be able to walk after he finishes with me.

"Sweet Lilly, you have everyone fooled." I hear the smile on his face as he makes that statement. I know I'm a closet naughty girl, but I've been dying to break out and enjoy. Leaning forward, I pull on his bottom lip with my teeth and wrap my hands around his neck. I've managed to get exactly where I want to be without having to climb up his body. The movements of my hips show him that I'm begging for him to move this along.

He is filling me up beyond comprehension as he begins to enter me and I want more. I want to have *all* of him in me. That will mean we are completely connected and this is something I crave. I need him. All of him. Right now. I rotate my hips and try to work my way down his extremely large erection.

He works with me, rotating and slowly driving upward at the same time I rotate downward. His piercing hits my entrance and it takes a deep, hard thrust for him to enter me completely. We both stop moving and this gives me a chance to accept the burn of him stretching me. It's a delicious pain that I welcome. No one has ever filled me so entirely before and tears fill my eyes from the realization that this is finally happening.

"You still with me?" His breath brushes over my lips with the closeness of his words.

"Yeah."

"You're so fucking tight right now." His heavy breath hits my face in perfect timing with my own leaving my body. I want him to move, but I'm afraid for him to at the same time. If he moves, I may lose it and be known as the girl that can't handle him in this way. I can feel that he is getting ready to tear me apart and it will have nothing to do with the size of his dick.

I pull his face into mine and start to kiss him. He returns my eagerness and passion with his kiss. I've waited so long for this moment and don't want to rush this.

Chapter Two

Luke

Her piercings have me turned the fuck on. I'm ready to do this. She's rotating her hips again, just begging for me to get on with it. I know this is wrong and that I'll pay for this one day. The boys will have my ass, but this is going to be worth everything they throw my way.

I hold her legs and begin to move slowly in and out of her. She is extremely tight and I can immediately tell this is going to be tricky as hell. Her moan in my ear has me slowing my thrusts until she can take me all the way. It's killing me to stop and wait for her to adjust, but I refuse to hurt her. Everything pauses. We are both frozen in movement and I can feel her stretching to accept me.

Her hands hold my face in place and she starts to kiss me again. Her lips are so fucking soft and I dive straight into her kiss. How many hours have I spent watching these lips, trying to convince myself that she was off limits and not worth the backlash of the Walker boys? Too. Fucking. Many.

Her nipple piercings are pressed against my chest and I welcome the scrape of the metal. I can feel her heat through the condom and it's driving me fucking crazy. With my hands braced on the wall beside her body, I begin to move in and out of her tightness. Her sounds echo my own and we are quickly reaching the point that will send us both over the edge.

I can hear someone near the door, so I pause and move in to cover her, trying to keep anyone from fucking seeing her gorgeous tits. Her breath hits my ear as she fucking begins to nibble. I can't concentrate on who's at the damn door and I don't give a shit anymore. This girl is driving me crazy. Our noises grow louder. Slapping. Moaning. Groaning. Heavy Breathing. She eventually screams my fucking name when she bursts over the edge. *That has to be the sexiest sound that I've ever heard come out of her mouth.*

"Shit, you are so fucking sexy." Our breathing is still erratic and out of control, and I pull on one of her nipple piercings just slightly with my teeth and feel her start to rotate again.

"You're trying to kill me." Her words are a breathy whisper near my ear. Her breath hitches as I tug on the other piercing.

"Death by orgasm. That's not such a bad way to go."

"Hmmmm. No, it's not." I love the sound of her moans as she tries to talk. We are still connected and I reach my hand between us to flick her clit piercing. Her sudden intake of air tells me she wants it again. I don't plan to leave her wanting. In fact, I want her so satisfied she doesn't need any for a very long time.

I rub her clit without mercy until she has no comprehension of even her own name. Listening to the sound of her coming undone for the fourth time has me fucking hard again in no time. Fuck. *Will we ever be able to walk out of this room?*

The sound of our bodies connecting as I pump every last ounce of myself into her is something that I'll never forget. There are girls that just fit and the movements match. She has *definitely* made her way to the top of my list of girls that can meet me thrust for thrust.

Our orgasms crash hard simultaneously and the guilt follows. I've fucked up. There's no way I can keep my hands off of her in the future. This was supposed to be a one time thing. Hell, we haven't even left the tiny fucking closet and that one-time shit has been blown out of the fucking water.

My body tenses up as I start to over analyze what has happened. She senses my change and stiffens as well.

"No strings attached, Luke. I don't expect anything from you that you aren't willing to give." Her words are meant to soothe me. *Why is it... they don't*? It's exactly what I want to hear from her, so why do her words piss me off?

"No strings attached," I repeat her uncommitted way of calming me.

She begins to move her legs from around my hips, so I pull out of her and guide her to a standing position. Her legs are unsteady and she falls back into the wall.

"You okay?

"I'm good. No worries." I can feel the awkwardness as we stand there. This is another reason we should never have gone there. We have to act normal in front of everyone and I'm worried this will change everything. *Can we really be friends with benefits?*

The sloppy condom reminds me of the mess I just made. If only the real mess was as easy to clean up as this, I'd be good.

I hear Taron laughing through the door and decide that it's time to do damage control. He's laughing now, but he'll be fucking psychotic if he sees this scene.

"I'm going out first. You take your time. I'll try to divert the guys' attention so you can slip out," I whisper against her lips before I kiss her one last time.

"Okay. Thanks." Her voice is even softer than normal and I almost don't hear her reply.

With the condom in hand, I exit the room only to find a mic right outside the door and Taron sitting on the large speaker laughing his ass off.

The irony of the situation makes me smile until I hear the sound of Lilly's sniffling blaring through the speaker. I charge straight to the cord attached to the wall, providing the electricity for Taron's fucking amusement. The cord flies across the room from the force of my aggression as I yank it out of the fucking wall.

What an ass. The urge to put him in his place is overridden by my respect for Lilly.

"Damn, boy. Slappin' that ass in high volume! Your girl of the day sure enjoyed your moves."

"Fuck off, Taron."

"Oh, come on! That shit was great! I amplified your sex sounds throughout the whole fucking room! How does it feel to have an audience listening in?" He continues to laugh. Damn, it takes every bit of control not to throw this right back at him and tell him it was Lilly, the girl he considers his fucking 'cousin', that I just had screaming my name. *That* would shut his ass up.

"Hopefully you learned something, you sick bastard." I choose to bite my tongue and just take what he dishes out. There is no way I'm telling him who just got me off twice in record time. *Fuck. How am I going to deal with her every day?*

Lilly

No regrets. No strings attached.

Just raw sex that is long overdue and better than I dreamed possible. He knows how to melt a girl and turn her into someone she hardly recognizes. He made me feel so good, and I know it's something he has experience doing. His contact list of hookup girls is longer than my entire friend list. Now I understand why girls come back for more. Once you have a taste of this man, you want more. No matter what agreements or non-committed understandings you have to make. No strings attached? *No problem, just give it to me like you did last time.*

Nothing like my legs going weak on me after he finished working me over. Luke is sexy as hell—I knew it would be that good with him. I start to relive what just happened, knowing it'll probably be one of the few times he'll actually hook up with me before I become too attached, if it's not already too late for that. I've spent a year working with him and watching him. We were just as explosive as I thought we would be. I also know he isn't interested in any type of relationship with me.

The realization of what I've just done to my heart begins to wash over me. How can I spend time with him like I have to and not want more with him? How will I handle him hooking up with another girl?

My entire body feels empty now that he's walked out. I let the tears fall as I start to search for my clothes. Knowing I can't talk to anyone about this, and trying to figure out how to act like my world wasn't just flipped upside down, is just a little too much for me to handle right now. The only light I have is from my cell phone; luckily this room is small enough that this works.

I find my panties just as I hear the door knob turn. I freeze in position, hoping that whoever it is doesn't flip on the light. His voice travels right through me.

"Just want to make sure you can get out of here without anyone seeing you." I don't get a chance to respond before he is right up next to me again. "And to say that we aren't finished here. Consider that foreplay for what I have planned for you." His breath hits my ear as his words burn through me. *Can he get any sexier?*

Waiting for his next move is excruciating. I want him to touch me, but it has to be what *he* wants to do. I've seen him get irritated with the girls always nagging for more attention. Luke is an 'in the moment' kind of guy, and if he isn't feeling it, then it won't be happening.

Finally, he runs his hands down my arms, sending chills over me again. "When did you get so damn sexy? I can't keep my fucking hands off of you tonight." He has my mind in so much chaos that I choose not to say a word and just relish this moment.

"I want to spend the night with you in your hotel room."

"Okay." My quiet voice stops his hands from roaming even further across my skin. His touch almost burns me and his fingers grip my hips as he pulls me against him.

"Feel what you do to me." Does he think I could miss it? Luke is *definitely* not lacking in that department. I push back against him to encourage him even more and listen to his breath hitch. We move together just enough to tease us both.

Luke has no idea how much I'm into him. If he did, none of this would be happening. He would keep a major distance from me if he knew my heart is already falling for him. I know him well enough to know this, so I have to keep my true feelings inside and just see where all of this goes.

"Feel what you do to me." I pull his hand lower until he is rubbing my piercing. His laughter fills my ear and I let go of his hand. He doesn't remove it, but instead continues my torture.

"Aren't you a naughty one? If people only knew the real you." I know what he's saying. I hold back in life. He makes me want to live and take chances. I don't know what it is about him that makes me feel like I can be as expressive as I want, but I can with everything *except* my true feelings for him.

"I'm glad you find humor in me trying to be sexy."

"Trying? There's no trying. You've *nailed* sexy and I can't wait to see more." I bend over to get my jeans and grab one of the hotel key cards out of the pocket. Turning to face him, I reach and put my hand in his back pocket, leaving the card behind when I pull my hand out. I don't miss the opportunity to squeeze his ass in the process.

"You have my key. If you want to see more, then you know where to find me." I can literally feel his smile when he pulls me in for a kiss.

"Let me leave the room first. I'll distract the guys again so you can exit without anyone seeing you. They'll have my ass if they find out it's you in here."

"Okay. Thanks." I start to pull my jeans on. He pulls away while I finish dressing, and then with one last kiss, he turns and walks toward the door.

I don't hear anyone, so I open the door in time to catch him walking down the hall. His swagger reminds me why it's so easy to fall for him. He's just a confident guy who knows how to have fun. I wish I had his confidence, but it's something I'm working on. I wait until he turns the corner before I look behind me.

"Well, well, well. What do we have here?" That would be Ivy's voice causing my instant panic. I turn to see both of the girls and just know Ivy and Eaven will see it on my face instantly.

"What do you mean?"

"Bullshit! Don't even try to hide the fact that your hair is fucked. You *look* fucked. Not to mention the way you were looking at him walk away. We know what's going on." I decide not to even try to deny it. I just smile.

"I don't kiss and tell."

'What about fuck and tell?" Leave it up to Ivy to get right down to the details. Eaven smacks Ivy's arm after she asks me.

We all start laughing and I want to tell them, but I can't. Luke is related to Eaven and that would be terrible for her, not to mention I need this to stay on the down low until I decide if it's worth telling the Walkers.

"Not that, either."

"Oh! Thank God! I don't want to hear about my cousin."

"He's not *my* cousin! I want to know once and for all if he's as hung as he acts like he is." Ivy's stance is that of someone impatiently waiting to be answered. My smile hasn't fallen and I realize how much I've missed these girls.

"Well? Spill it! I want to know if Luke is the Mandingo he thinks he is."

"Ivy, I'm going to hurt you if she describes details. I don't want to know."

"Then walk away, Ev. We have business to discuss here." I watch the two of them interact and actually feel a ping of jealousy at how close they are. These two have been through so much together and have always been there for each other. There's no doubt if trouble were to find one of them that the other would jump in immediately to help. I've never had a bond like that with another female.

My closest friends growing up were the Walkers. Our families lived close and the guys have always felt the need to take care of me. It's never gone beyond a brotherly love from any of them, but there have been times that I've had to call one of them to help me out of a situation.

They've referred to me as a cousin for years, but the reality is... we aren't even related. Their protective nature probably stems from the first time I met them. They walked up on a kid from our grade school harassing me one day. Needless to say, when they were finished with him, I never had any other problems growing up. It was very well known that if you mess with Lilly, the Walkers will unleash hell *all over* your ass.

I bring my attention back to the girls and see them both looking at me like I'm crazy.

"Are you trying to avoid the question?" Ivy keeps pressing while Eaven starts to walk off. I decide to have a little fun with the girls and I may as well enjoy the banter while I can.

"Let's just say he probably wasn't exaggerating."

"OH MY GOD. I can hear you! Seriously!" Ev begins to walk faster away from us. Ivy sends me a little wink while looking proud as hell. I'm not sure if she's pleased that I gave up a few details or the fact that he's as hung as she expected.

"Don't worry, we'll keep this from the guys until you have a chance to see if there's something to announce."

"I appreciate it. We're just having fun and I don't need the added stress from anyone else blowing this out of control." She leans in for a hug and pulls me in tight.

"I didn't get a chance to tell you thanks for helping with the nursery. It turned out perfect and I love it. I know you had a huge part in finishing it up."

"Of course. I enjoyed helping Taron out."

"It was so nice to come home from the hospital to the nursery being ready!"

"Speaking of which, where is that cutie?"

"She's with her daddy. I just finished feeding her and he wanted to show her off to the rest of the crew that hasn't seen her yet."

"This show tonight will be loud for her."

"Oh, don't worry. Taron has everything covered. He bought her some ear muffs to buff out some of the sound and also has a room for me to use if I need to feed her or slip away. He's kind of out of control with his protecting us, but I love him for it."

"Awww. You can tell he loves her."

"Yes. I couldn't have picked a better dad for her." I watch her face falter just a bit and I'm curious why.

"Are you happy, Ivy?" She looks stunned at my question. I can see her wheels turning as I wait for her answer.

"Yes, I'm happy. I love him and he's a great father to Heaven."

"Okay. I was just making sure."

"I really do love him. I'm just trying to figure out how our forever will turn out before I jump all the way in."

"Sometimes you have to jump before you can see the clear picture." My words hit her and she looks over at Taron walking toward us. I know these two are meant for each other—there's no doubt to *anyone* that knows them. I guess I'll wait like the rest of the world to see how it all turns out.

"Hey, baby." Taron moves in for a kiss from Ivy, not even caring that I'm standing right here. I want what they have. Why should I remain single and never get to have this with someone?

Chapter Three

Luke

I've seriously fucked up. It's about time to go on stage and I have to pull my shit together and act normal. Lilly's boldness just has me surprised and I have to say that I'm genuinely intrigued. What else will she be up for? If the closet incident was any indication, I'm sure it will only get better.

I should stay away, but I don't plan to until we've had a little more fun. I pull out my guitar and begin tuning it when Talon walks up.

"I heard you on the big speakers. Luke, remember we have the girls here. Try to keep your skanks away from them." *Damn it. This is going to be torture.* At least he's not being a complete ass like Taron was.

"I'll work on that." Keeping it short and simple is the best way around this. I try to stay focused on my warm-up when Lilly walks in. She struts over to her case and I have to watch her ass the whole time—there's just no way around it. She isn't making eye contact with me and I have to give her credit for her performance. If I didn't know what she had just done, I'd never guess.

Talon's grumble followed by an insane amount of noise from his set distracts me. I purposely don't look over at him, knowing that was meant for me. I walk over to her just as she starts to play. We have a pre-show ritual and I lead us straight into it. We always work the crowd together. She is amazing when it comes to this. Her demeanor on stage is pretty much like I just had the privilege of witnessing in person. She has no problem putting on a show for the fans. Her moves catch my eye every show and I love how she can match me while we play. She's a badass and there really aren't very many guitarists I would say that about.

Her smile when I reach her tells me she's as ready as I am to be back on stage. It's been a while since we've been on the road. The court battles that Ivy and Taron have been fighting have taken every ounce of attention from the whole Walker family. Lilly and I have done a few shows together at some small venues, but for the most part we focused on the new record. Tonight we will encore three of our new songs and we're all itching to step out on stage again.

I enjoy hanging with Lilly. It seems we're constantly together, working or trying to plan something for the band. She works hard and so do I, even though it may seem that I'm all play. This gig means a lot to me and I want it to work just as much as the others do.

We begin to move our equipment onto the stage and work with the crew to set up the final prep before the show. Lilly moves offstage and my desire to follow her is pissing me off. I resist the urge and choose to watch instead. She moves to stand with Ivy and Ev. I look up at Eaven and see her staring me down like I'm in trouble. I flash a smile and look away, knowing I'm going to be hearing from her soon.

I move backstage to wait for show time. The sound of the music from the other band begins and I start to watch her. She looks so carefree with her hands in the air and her hips moving with the music. I want more than anything to bump right up behind her and feel her every move.

She glances my way and I let her see me watching her. This only encourages her to dance even sexier. She's still standing with the girls, but she's behind them while they watch the show from the side.

Her hip movements are going to be the death of me.

Lilly

I know he's watching me—I can feel it. His stare always does something to me. If he doesn't stop, I'm going to walk back there and attack him while everyone watches.

If he's going to stare like this, I may as well give him a show. Adding a little more rotation to my sway, I really start to get into the music. I feel strong arms come around me and pull me backward into all over hardness. I'd know these arms anywhere.

I don't stop dancing; I even grind a little harder back into him intentionally. My heels make me the perfect height to make this work to my advantage. We move together, not caring who's watching. I turn to face him and wrap my arms around his neck. He moves his hands down my back and over my ass.

He tries to say something in my ear, but the music is too loud for me to hear it. His lips brush across my ear and I lean my head to the side to prevent the chills from rising again.

I continue to move against him, but he doesn't really join in. I feel someone brush up against me. Ivy moves in, along with Eaven, and they both begin to dance near Luke and me. I have a feeling they are trying to make this situation seem less than it really is.

I have to love these girls for trying to keep everything calm even when Luke and I are about to combust. Unfortunately, I'm going to have to have a talk with the Walkers real soon about Luke. It's not like we'll be in a relationship or anything, but I want to be able to be comfortable around him. I'm sure shit will hit the fan when they find out I'm good with just having fun with Luke.

I watch Luke's face while the music continues. His smirk is ridiculously sexy, making me ready to feel his mouth on me again. Being this close to him is affecting me more than I'd like to admit. My movements against his body seem to be amusing him and I love watching his reactions. His playful expression tells me he's enjoying himself.

The song ends so I stop moving. He pulls me in close at the hips and I pull my face away from his a little. I pull my bottom lip between my teeth and his eyes move to my lips. He watches them closely and it seems so bold to be this close.

The next song comes on and I notice Talon moving toward us. I pull my arms away from Luke before Talon gets too close to us. Standing close to him for the remainder of the songs before we take the stage is a challenge. My mind is filled with what I want to do with him. You wouldn't think we'd just gone at it not that long ago. I've been attracted to him for almost a year now. Having a sample of what he's like has just made this worse.

We start to take the stage and he leans in to my ear before I begin to play "Let me see you shake that ass. Tease me with it and remind me what I will be hitting tonight."

"You seem pretty sure of yourself."

"You know it's happening." *Hell yes it's happening.* I wouldn't miss it for anything right now. He has me hot and bothered, knowing what I have to look forward to.

Talon starts playing the beat on the drums in the spotlight, drawing all the screams in the crowd. Luke and I meet in the center of the dark stage, back to back, and begin our thunderous intro before Taron moves out into the light. Looking out into the crowd, I see the faces of the fans that are so happy to see us again. This is what it's all about. These people genuinely missed us. It feels great to be a part of this group of talented guys.

We begin the show with an encore presentation of one of our new songs and it goes over insanely well. This is the song Talon changed up late in the recording, adding the flare it needed. With Taron's voice and our thunder, there is no way this song isn't going to be a huge hit.

We get through the show without any complications. The crowd seems to love all of our new songs. Luke and I were a great combo out there. I love when everything goes down without a flaw. It puts everyone in a great mood and we can have a ton of fun afterward.

We move out to greet some of the fans and Holden is on me tight with security. That is something that will *never* be taken lightly. The team that the guys have put together is a great group of guys. Holden runs the show without a doubt. Aiden has become his sidekick in the business and it's great to know we're protected. The guys are doing it very inexpensively for us on this tour until we can get on our feet even more. I know the Walker parents have helped with protection. They want the new women in their family to be completely safe. Not to mention lil' Heaven is here now, too.

I move to pull in some pictures and programs to autograph and in the process get surrounded by fans. The guys move in quick to keep them at a distance. Glancing over at Luke, I notice him watching me. His sexy smirk has me smiling back in no time. I can't wait to suck on those lips again.

Hoping no one notices our chemistry for a little while, I try to focus solely on the fans. It's hard when I crave his touch like I do. I'm going to pass this off as not getting my fill of the man I've had my eye on for so long. His eagerness to hook up again has surprised me and I hope it isn't going to ruin me.

We finish with the last of the fans and I move backstage to get my stuff. He moves with me, his eagerness matching mine. I pull my case up so I can pack the only thing I need to walk out of here. As I'm placing my guitar in the case, he moves in behind me. His breath on my back spikes a line of chills up my back. I know it's just a matter of time before one of the guys sees him doing this to me. Making a mental note to tell them about us in the morning, I close my case with a snap.

"You ready for this?" His hand moves across my side and pulls my hip toward him until we are flush up against each other. *Hell yes, I'm ready.*

"If you think you can handle more." I'm not sure who is more turned on here. We are both about to explode and you can feel the heat between us. I move to the side and reach for his case, handing it to him as I turn and walk off. He's following—I can feel him.

We get on the empty bus, knowing the others will be coming soon. We could go on without everyone, but that would definitely put up a red flag about us. If we want to stay on the down low a little longer, we need to try to keep it together until we get to the hotel. I set my stuff down and make myself at home in my usual spot. He flops down next to me, making sure to sit as close as possible to me.

He turns to kiss me and I welcome him. This man knows what to do with his tongue. I can feel his facial hair when I brush my hands over his face, pulling him in tighter. Honestly, I never took him for the type to enjoy kissing this much. His fingers begin to roam across my skin, but never reach the areas I ache for him to touch. The feeling across my skin as it becomes alive for the umpteenth time tonight is incredible. He's going to make it impossible for me to forget him. *Why does he have to be so damn good at this?*

Chapter Four

Luke

Yet again, I can't keep my hands off of her. It was such a bad idea to taste the temptation that has been haunting me for months. Knowing where we're headed tonight is driving me crazy. I have no intentions of sleeping and neither will she if *I* have any say about it. We can sleep tomorrow on the drive. Luckily, it's only about a five-hour drive tomorrow, so we don't have to leave at the ass crack of dawn.

Running my fingers over her seems to be making her as insane as I am. I pull my hand away just in time for the door to swing open. Ivy and Eaven step in and both begin the stare down.

"You two are ridiculous. Get a room." Eaven seems a little irritated. I decide not to move from Lilly, knowing the talk from Eaven is near. She moves to the back of the bus with all of the baby stuff loading her arms. Ivy moves forward with Heaven and hands her to me to hold before she moves to the back of the bus.

Holding a baby isn't exactly what I had in mind right now, but I really don't have a choice. This little girl has the darkest head of hair and her tiny lips are already proving to be full. Her eyes are bright and she has full lashes. I know those two will have their hands full with this tiny bundle. It's bad when you don't know which parent you hope she acts like in the future. The two of them are a riot, but it's not something you want to think about a baby becoming.

Lilly moves in closer to talk to Heaven. I watch her face light up as she talks in a different voice. Heaven's face lights up and she begins to make her own sounds. Her arms begin to move slightly with her excitement to see Lilly.

"Do you want to hold her?"

"Nah. You've got her." I pull her up to my chest and wrap her tighter in her blanket. Her eyes light up and I swear she smiles at me. The only problem is, it's followed by the horrible smell of baby shit.

"Really, lil' babe? You had to poop on Uncle Luke?" Why is it her smile is even larger now? I can tell we are going to have many moments like this as she grows up. You can't help but fall for this tiny bundle.

"Ivy, you have a mess to clean up."

"What, you don't do diapers?"

"Hell no, I don't wipe asses no matter *how* cute they are." Standing up, I hand Heaven over to Ivy. She puts a blanket down beside where I was sitting and begins to undress Heaven. I look back and see Eaven smiling—she knows I'd rather listen to her than smell baby shit, so I take the plunge and start walking.

"I hope you're careful. You need to watch yourself, Luke. If you screw her over, the guys will never forgive you. Everything is finally falling into place and you need to be thinking with the head on top of your body, not the one leading you around."

"Thanks for your concern, but we're just having fun. We both understand this is a no strings attached hookup, and I'm pretty sure I gave the Walkers the benefit of the doubt when it came to you and Ivy."

"You did not! I had to tell you where to stick it when it came to Talon."

"I know you did, but I stepped back and let you two fall in love without complications. I'm not saying that's what will happen here, but only time will tell. Right now, it's all for fun."

"Well, the guys are going to shit if they find out you are screwing around with everyone *including* Lilly. You know how close they are to her."

"Yes, I'm aware they don't want anyone near her. She isn't the innocent little girl they see her as. I'll handle the guys."

"Luke, please be careful. I know you just want to have fun and the tour is just starting. It'll be a long tour if you mess this up."

Pulling her in for a hug, I try to ease her mind. "I'll be careful. You worry about keeping your man happy and off my ass." I can see Lilly watching me and the look on her face tells me she's deep in thought. I hope to hell she isn't changing her mind about tonight.

"I had better go help the guys load up the rest of the equipment." I let my eyes meet Lilly's as I walk past. Her small smirk gives me very little hope that she's still with me about tonight.

Jumping out of the bus, I hear the guys coming.

"Where have you been, asshole? This equipment doesn't walk itself out here." Talon is leading the group, everyone carrying as much as they can. I open the storage doors and begin to help loading the gear. This really isn't the best way to start out the tour. Trying to stay focused on the band may prove difficult, but it's something that I've got to do.

"Here with the girls. Heaven ran me out of there with a shit bomb."

"Good. She was due for a poop." I look at Taron and I can't help but be confused. How did Taron not only get tamed, but flattened so much that timing his baby's poop is a normal thing? Such a rock god thing to do.

"I don't even know how to respond to that, dude."

"What? My girl has been constipated and she needed that." This gets him looks from all of the crew except Talon. Everyone busts out laughing and it doesn't even faze Taron.

"All of you can fuck off. I wouldn't trade my life with any of you fuckers." It's funny to see him like this. He used to be my partner in crime when it came to hooking up with the ladies. Ivy put a stop to all that long before they even became a couple. He fell for her hard—almost as hard as Talon fell for Eaven.

Traveling with these couples is going to be a real hitch in my single lifestyle. Lilly and I will just have to make the best of it.

Our trip to the hotel is short. We don't waste time checking in and I go ahead and move my stuff into the room I've booked. In an effort to save some money, I'm splitting this room with Aiden. This guy is a trip. He works security for us in a rock and roll setting, wearing a cowboy hat and shit kickers. It's hard not to respect a man that doesn't change who he truly is, no matter the situation. He was really there to help Ivy during the worst time in her life. If Taron can let it all go and bring him into our circle, then I have no right to not fully accept him as he is.

Grabbing my cell phone to text Lilly, I move to open my bag to get my shower stuff. Wiping away all of the sweat and filth from the fans is crucial before I move in on Lilly.

Luke: What room?

Lilly: Let's talk.

Luke: Ok. What room?

Lilly: 229

Luke: I'll be there after my shower.

Lilly: I'm taking one too, so give me some time.

Luke: You have 'til I get out, then I'm beating down the door.

Let's talk. I don't like the sound of that. This is supposed to be uncomplicated and easy. I like her, she likes me. We don't have to please anyone else.

I don't rush in the shower, giving her enough time to do what she needs. I'm glad there aren't any other single women on the tour so she isn't sharing a room. That would complicate the hell out of things. Aiden looks at me suspiciously when I start for the door in only my shorts.

"Don't wait up on me. I have a key."

"Man. Make sure you know what you're doing." I don't even reply to him. I don't have to answer to people if I want to hook up with someone who is eager and willing. Lilly and I are both grown adults and all of these warnings are pissing me off.

Walking down the hall, I can hear Heaven crying in one room and Talon talking in another. Her room is all the way to the end, so I move quickly, hoping to make it past all of their rooms without a situation erupting.

Why do I feel like a teenager sneaking around again? This is bullshit.

I knock on the door and she instantly opens it up. Her tank top and short shorts are so different than anything I've seen her in. She manages sexy in every way. Propping the door open with an extended arm, her eyes scan my entire body. I know she appreciates the view by the way she takes me in.

My tattoos are very unique and well-placed, usually getting the approval of most of the ladies. There are some haters and people who wonder what I'll do when I'm old and wrinkled. My only response is that I'll kick it with my other tattooed friends and we'll be wrinkled together.

"What are we talking about?" I stroll past her and lie across her bed, knowing she'll have a rough time talking to me in bed.

She stands at the foot of the bed and begins to take me in again. I let her look and wait for her to say something or jump into this bed and let us do our best talking. She continues to stay still, only letting her eyes move.

"You going to stand there or climb my ladder and come with me?" I watch for a smile that I know is coming. Her face lights up and I begin to laugh at her shocked expression.

"Really, Luke?"

"Don't pretend you're not ready to climb on top of me and give it to me just like I want."

"I didn't say I wasn't, but I want to make sure we have an understanding here." She has me intrigued.

"Okay. What do I need to understand to get inside those shorts?"

"You need to understand that this is just us having fun. The Walkers will give us hell if they see you acting like you did tonight. I don't want to have to fight with them over us."

"Agreed."

"Besides, I could tell Eaven didn't approve of us." I see her face fall as she begins to talk.

"Ev was just threatening me not to mess this up with you. She knows the guys will flip their shit."

"Well, there isn't anything to mess with. We both know this is just a hookup, so we're good."

"I love how you're talking. So quit and get over here."

It's time to move this along. I want to feel her mouth on me.

Lilly

How long have I waited for this control? To have him in my bed, begging for me to join him. I want to lick his six-pack abs all the way up to his gorgeous lips. There is one thing that will happen tonight... I *will* be exploring his endless tattoos. Holy shit, the definition of his muscles offset by the brightly colored tats is obviously a weakness for me. *Control, Lilly. Don't jump on the bed like an excited fan would.*

I turn to sit on the edge of the bed, slightly facing him. He moves for me, instantly kissing my neck as he slides the spaghetti strap off my shoulders. I didn't even bother with a bra, knowing this was going to happen tonight. His hands slide over my chest and around each of my breasts. His slight tug on both piercings has me at his mercy just that quick. *Damn him.*

I let his hands consume me and he eventually moves to stand in front of me. Sitting on the bed, I'm faced with the abs I've watched from afar all these months. The urge to lean forward and run kisses over each bump wins over. With the light on, I can see everything. Right over the top of his waistband is a tattoo of brass knuckles. He stands there and lets me slowly move my fingers over each ring. I notice how each ripple of his muscle is defined and his skin is just a complete work of art. Sliding my hands up his stomach, I look up into his eyes and begin to run my lips over the same tattoo my fingers just explored.

With a slip of my tongue, I move to the next tattoo. His eyes follow me as I leave a trail of moisture and begin to kiss the endless ink around his body. He remains still during my attack and I take time to appreciate all the detail. His back is completely covered in numerous individual tats—all connected—creating one massive full jacket of ink. His tattoo artist must be top notch to pull of this symmetry and color along with the intricate detail that has gone into each one.

He turns his head to watch me. I've never seen anything like it. Sure, he has been around without a shirt on—after all it's Luke I'm talking about—but looking this closely is a whole new experience.

"How many hours do you have into them?"

"More than one hundred hours."

"It's breathtaking to see them this close."

"Yeah, I know." I move my fingers over the contours of his back. His skin erupts in goose bumps as I slide my fingertips across his shoulders. Running my hands down each of his arms, I pass over the bulk of his biceps and it's honestly even more of a turn on to feel them in the flesh. His sleeves are always tight and I'm always tortured to reach out and touch the muscles fighting to break free from the material confining them.

I'm met with a smirk when I make it around to face him.

"My turn. Clothes off." His demand is sexy as hell. My body craves him, so there's no way I'm denying him. I start to slide my tank down over my hips, dragging my shorts along with it. My g-string panties don't do much to cover me up, but that's all that's left to hide behind.

My nipples ache from our earlier play, and when he rubs up against them it causes me to pull back just a little. He seems to take notice and begins to move more sensually over each of them. His tongue moves strategically around each nipple and his hands move around to grab my entire ass. He's taller than me, but not by much, so this seems to be working well.

He edges me to the bed so I climb on. Lying on my stomach, I watch him climb over me. The touch of his hands as he runs them over me feels so good. I let him massage my back and wherever else his hands roam. *God, he's so good at this.*

He moves to straddle my legs and leans over to kiss my back. I can feel his facial hair brushing over my skin. Closing my eyes, I take in all of the sensations that he's causing. He smells so damn good. I already know he looks fucktastic, and holy hell if he doesn't feel great, too. His breathing near my ear is a complete turn on. That leaves taste as a sensation that I need to explore more of.

He moves off of me, pulling me with him once he's on his back. I slide in next to him and he invades my mouth with his tongue. His kiss is something else, making it nearly impossible to pull away from him.

His erection springs free as I begin to slide his shorts down his legs. Leaning up on my knees, I remove them completely and toss them off the bed. He moves the pillow to prop himself up and watches me lower my mouth to cover his dick. His width, combined with the metal of the piercings, makes this interesting.

Sliding down further in the bed, I adjust myself so that I'm on my knees between his legs. Looking into his eyes, I run my tongue up his entire length, applying pressure on the underside. His resolve is broken when I shift my tongue so that my piercing finishes off the trail. He closes his eyes and exhales loudly, running his palm over the back of my head. This is his way of encouraging me to take him all in.

I hate the sound of teeth on metal, so I work my lips and tongue over him, sucking on the way back up. He has three bars on the underside of his dick, so it is definitely a task to do this quietly. If there has ever been a moment of too much metal in one space, I'm sure this is it. I decide a slow pace is how to keep this under control.

Watching his face during my attack is a complete turn on. I can see want and desire in his eyes. His eyes move to my ass when I lower my head again and I can't wait to feel him behind me.

Luke is not only a shower, but he's also a fucking *grower*. Getting this close to him and his size makes me wonder how the hell he even fit inside me earlier.

"Back up to the edge of the bed." His order makes my insides flutter in anticipation. I move slowly while he slides off the bed. The sound of the condom wrapper means I won't have to wait much longer. There isn't any preparation needed on my part. I'm apparently a sopping wet mess when it comes to this man being near me.

His hands around my hips, pulling me closer, remind me just how strong yet gentle he is. After he positions me, he pauses just enough to run his hands over my ass cheeks.

"What I would give to get a hold of this ass." There is no way I'm letting his dick anywhere *near* my ass. *Are you kidding me?* He would ruin me. I look over my shoulder at him and see his huge smile on his face. He runs his tongue over his lower lip quickly and then proceeds forward to fill me completely.

His slow entry gives me a chance to adjust again. This position is even deeper, and I have to remind myself to breathe at first. His piercings pull me even tighter once they enter. He finally has to grab both of my shoulders to drive in the final few inches.

All comprehension is lost again. I know nothing except the pleasure-pain that I'm experiencing. He pulls out slowly only to thrust in harder all the way. A moan escapes my mouth and is quickly replaced by another when he begins to move in and out of me with a rhythm that leaves me no time to react. His balls slap my clit piercing, and I swear it's like a knock on the door to the best orgasm of my life.

His grip on my shoulders allows for the hard, deep sex I know we both want. I scream through my first orgasm and he doesn't slow down. He moves to rotate his hips slightly with every entry creating a whole new feeling and I'm losing it again.

My head drops from exhaustion and he bundles my hair into his grip, pulling until his mouth is right over my ear.

"We are not even *close* to being done tonight."

Chapter Five

Luke

This night is going to be the death of us both. She's not supposed to feel this good. I need to be able to walk away from her and not itch for this again.

Gripping her long hair in one hand and a shoulder in the other, I thrust on until I'm filling my condom with my release. She manages a third orgasm that sends her lifeless, face-first on the bed when I let her go.

I throw the condom in the trash and grab a towel to clean up. She begins to crawl up the bed and I know I've done my job. She's done for a while. I always take care of the ladies first. Climbing on to the other side of the bed, I pull the covers over her and sprawl out for some great after sex sleep.

I wake up to her naked chest on my back while she is tracing some of my tattoos. This is a great way to wake up. I can only think of a couple ways that could top this. Rolling over, I pull her on top of me. Her tits are gorgeous and I need to spend some time on them.

If I didn't have my hands on them, I'd think they were fake. That's definitely something I can distinguish upon inspection. Hers are perfectly sized and ready for my mouth to explore. She moves to straddle me and I enjoy the view. The room is lit from the lights we left on last night. I glance over at the curtain and see that it's still dark outside.

"What time is it?"

"Time for round two." Her response surprises me and I can't hide the laughter.

"What have I created?"

"You had nothing to do with what I've become."

"Oh really?"

"Yes. If you remember, I'm not a shy little virgin that you're transforming into a sex goddess. I'm already the sex goddess and you're just getting a taste." Sliding my hands up her body, I pull her down over me so I can give her tits the proper attention they deserve. She's sensitive when it comes to her nipples. I can tell by the way she gasps when I brush over them. She has a tattoo that runs up her side so I turn to look it over—I didn't take the time last night.

It's an upside down treble clef bumped up against a bass clef. Together they resemble a heart. Music notes travel down her side and I can't think of a more perfect tattoo for her.

She begins to move over me. This is that moment that sucks when the condom is clear across the room. Her movements aren't even needed because I woke up ready for this moment. She is hot as fuck and I plan to make sure I get as much of her as I can before daylight. I'm just glad she's on the same wave length.

"My condoms are in my shorts." I begin to lift up to move off the bed when she stops me.

"I have some right here." She holds up a row of the only condoms I'll use. She rips one off and tears it open with her teeth. Her hands roll it down my length and then she positions herself over me. I wait to see what she does.

She begins to slide down, but struggles to take it all in. I move to rub her clit, applying pressure on her piercing, causing her to stop moving all together. I quickly see this will be a long process if I let her run the show by herself. She moves her hips forward then back, solely looking for her own satisfaction.

I lead her upright and pull her down on me until I fill her again. Her head falls back so I sit up to wrap my arms around her. This position doesn't allow for much movement, but it's more about getting to know each other at this point. I know she's a second from exploding, so I freeze completely. An orgasm that's delayed is always so much better.

She moves on her own and manages to go off even without my help. This woman is hungry and full of sensations. Watching her face during her release is incredible. How many people get to see her like this? I know not many. She hides this and I love that she does. It's like opening a gift. You never know what's inside until you unwrap it.

She wraps both arms around my head and begins to kiss me deeply. Her push to send me back to the pillow is met with no resistance. She follows me and begins to move up and down on my cock. Her tightness and movements have me near release in no time. I let her work it, fighting the urge to take over the whole time. She moves faster and I can't take it anymore. Gripping her hips, I thrust up, pulling her down on me until I'm losing it again. I have no idea if she's pleased again—all rational thought was lost during the chaos of her unraveling me.

She leans up to pull my lip in for a kiss.

"Good mornin'!"

"I wish all mornings were like this." Her smile as she climbs off me falls when she looks at the clock.

"Shit, we have to leave in fifteen minutes."

"What? It's still dark outside."

"Yeah, Holden texted last night and told us we had to leave early because of a business meeting that came up."

"Shit." I rush around and grab my shorts. Pulling them on, I watch her move through the room completely naked. I burn this image into my head to remember at a later time. She turns on the water to the shower and I step into the bathroom to kiss her goodbye. She's looking in the mirror at herself when I open the door. Her face doesn't look like someone who is happy and just had numerous orgasms throughout the night.

"I'm going to go get my shower. I'll see you when we go down to the bus." She looks down at the sink as I approach her. I move in behind her and wait until she lifts her eyes into the mirror to look at me. Leaning in to place a kiss on her shoulder, I wrap my arms around her waist one last time before I walk out the door.

The hall is empty and I'm thankful for that. With my key in my hand, I head down the hall until I reach my room. Aiden isn't in the room when I arrive, which is a great thing. I hurry through the shower and get dressed in record time. It's a sweat pant and hoody type of day.

Most of the guys are near the bus. Taron is missing, but I'm sure he's going on no sleep with a baby in the room. Aiden walks up and doesn't say a word about me going missing in the night. It's nice to know he's got my back, or at the very least doesn't want to start crap with the Walkers.

When the girls arrive without Lilly, I start to worry about her. She usually beats Ev and Ivy out. I pull my phone out to text her just as she walks out of the lobby. She seems happier than she did before.

We all load the bus and she moves to sit in her normal seat. I do the same and sit across from her. She sits against the wall with her feet over the seat, puts her ear buds in, and lays her head back. Her indifference surprises me, but this works for me. It's good she won't be one of the clingers, wanting me to put a ring on it because we had one great night of sex.

I mirror her actions and lay back to catch some z's. It isn't long and we're on the road. This trip will seem like nothing compared to some of the road trips we go on.

I manage to catch up on my sleep and wake just as we arrive in Dallas. Lilly is still sleeping and it's funny just how worn out she looks. Her mouth is open and I can't resist the urge to pester her. Sliding across my seat, I lean over hers and scare her with my voice.

"Do you mind closing that sexy mouth of yours? You're giving me flashbacks that may end up causing a scene right here in this bus."

After her startled reaction, she smacks me on the arm and pushes me away.

"What the hell, Luke? I was sleeping good until you freaking woke me up." When I lean back up to move over to my seat, I notice Talon watching me over the seats. I don't give him any reaction, but I know a confrontation is coming soon.

We get to the venue and begin unloading the gear. I love how she's acting normal—I was afraid it would be awkward and cause a problem between us.

Our meeting goes well and we land five more venues for this tour. It seems like we'll be busy for about four weeks straight and then have a break for a couple of months.

Our show is about thirty minutes from starting, so I move to go backstage only to be stopped by Talon.

"I know you're watchin' yourself and that you don't need me to put you in your place."

"Not sure what you're talking about, but I'm good."

"You fucking know what I'm talking about. Lilly is *not* one of your whores." Hearing him say her name and whore in the same sentence does something to me. I get right in his face, nose to nose. My thoughts are all over the place as I try to find the exact words that I can actually say.

"What I do with Lilly is none of your fucking business."

"It becomes my business when you begin to fuck around while fucking her, which we know will happen."

"Fuck off, Talon."

"You don't deserve her." His intensity matches my own and I know this is not going to go well. Sadly, I can't disagree with him. She *does* deserve better. He shoves forward against my chest in a challenge for me to say anything else to set him off further.

Eaven pushes between us to face Talon. My eyes never leave his and his silent threat is very clear.

"Talon. What is wrong with you? You promised me that you'd leave it alone." Knowing Eaven is actually defending me warms me. I know this is huge for her to go against him, and I don't want this to cause a problem in their relationship, but he needs to butt out.

I turn to walk away only to become face to face with Taron. *Shit.*

"Is there a problem here?" Ivy is quick to pull his hand into hers and I just push past him. Nothing good will come of me trying to justify anything to them when I don't blame them for their actions. I have no desire to have a relationship right now, and she is someone they don't want to see get hurt. I understand that.

If she could only truly promise no strings, this won't get complicated, but apparently we have an obvious connection.

Hell, the fuckin' twins even noticed my attraction to her.

Lilly

Watching them all attack Luke pisses me off. He goes backstage to get away from everyone and I lay into the twins for their idiotic behavior.

"You have no right to interfere. There is nothing for you to worry about with Luke. Who I decide to hook up with has nothing to do with either of you, and I expect you to respect my privacy."

"Lilly, Luke couldn't keep it in his pants if he wanted to. You deserve better than that and I won't let him fuck you over." Talon has always been the more protective one over me. He demands that I'm given the respect I deserve, and in doing that he has scared off many of my potential guy friends.

"Talon. You stay out of this. I'm not young and dumb and I deserve the chance to have some fun." His face doesn't lighten up.

"I hope you have more respect for yourself than to spread your legs for someone who has probably been between *hundreds* of legs."

"Talon. If you don't stop right now, we will have a major issue." Eaven speaks up and moves in front of Talon's face. He looks down at her and doesn't seem too thrilled to be shut up about this.

"You don't have to worry about it. It's not like we've done anything anyway. Just chill the hell out. Luke isn't like that." He wants to say something, but the glare-down from Eaven has him pausing. I look for Taron and he doesn't seem to be as concerned with all of this. Holden looks pissed off, but isn't voicing his opinion.

"I'm a grown-ass woman and can do what I want. I never interfere with any of you and how you live your life. I want the same from you."

"Rebel Walking. How's it going? You guys look like you need to get laid." Garrett Riggins walks up with his cocky demeanor and places his arm over my shoulder. He's the drummer for 'Beckoning Reality', a band that's supposed to open for us at a few shows and we'll do the same for them. That's how we added five shows to the tour.

"Riggins, get your hands off of me before you lose function of those famous hands."

The surprise on his face is worth it until he leans in to whisper in my ear, "If you only knew just how famous these hands are, babe."

I return the gesture by whispering back to him, "Get your fucking hands off of me."

His facial reaction seems to challenge me and I feel his hand slide all the way down my back. Grabbing me on the ass, he starts to look around at everyone else. I pull away from him, knowing he's just trying to get a rise out of me. He's not usually this disgusting, but for some reason he's trying really hard today.

I look up and notice Luke watching. He doesn't seem to be bothered by Garrett manhandling me. That bothers me. Is it bad that I *want* him to be jealous? Luke isn't the jealous type, though—I knew this going into whatever it is we have going here.

Watching the Walker men stare down Garrett is more hysterical than anything else. These guys are hopeless. Don't get me wrong, I love that they care enough about me to try to protect me from the bad boys, but that's what I'm attracted to. I want a strong, tattooed guy who doesn't have to answer to anyone. You know... a guy like Luke.

Garrett moves in close to me again, making sure to run his hands over me once more. I let him, knowing the guys will have a rough time with it. They need to get over their protective nature, and I can't think of a better way than to force them to right in front of everyone here.

Luke turns to talk to a groupie and I lose track of what everyone is saying near me. I watch him flirt with her, knowing what's about to happen. It's like a train wreck that I can't turn my eyes from.

Chapter Six

Luke

I look over and see her face. It's full of disappointment, but I don't let her stop this. I pull tonight's blond honey closer to my body and fill my hands full of tight ass. It's nothing to get laid before the show. I do it regularly, so I'm not sure what her fucking deal is. This girl is nothing special. She's hot, but it's just a fuck. Besides that, she's letting that asshole grope her up and down right in front of everyone.

I move us into the bathroom to do the deed in private. It's another day in the life of a rocker. What can I say? I like boobs and vaginas.

She drops to her knees just like they all do. Her skills are lacking, and frankly, it irritates me so much I don't let her go on for very long. As soon as I hear her teeth clank against my metal, I pull her up from the floor.

Propping her on the cabinet, I don't waste time getting into position to finish this. I smile when I see yet another shocked expression. Every girl enjoys my Jacob's ladder piercing, but pair that with my size, and I get them every time. I pull her to the edge and she lifts her legs over my shoulders. This angle works perfectly and it doesn't take long for both of us to moan out in pleasure.

My moment is interrupted by someone banging on the door, so I pull my jeans back in place.

"What?"

"Showtime!" There's no mistaking that cocky voice is none other than Taron.

I leave tonight's lay behind and rush to the stage. I hear her strumming sharply. The sound of her bass guitar makes me feel just a little guilty, but it's what I do.

She's off limits. The Walker boys would have my ass if they only knew what I've done. It's for her own good anyway.

I step beside her on stage and she moves up to work the audience. I move up with her and the crowd goes wild when we work together. We know how to raise the noise level before a show. I watch her when she starts to move those damn hips. This is the part where I move back and watch the view—I fucking *love* this view.

We do our solos and work together through each song to put on the best show possible, just like we do every time.

As soon as the lights are cut, I move to the side of the stage and expect her to follow, but she doesn't. I start to look for her and eventually my eyes adjust enough to see her.

I watch her move in on him. She's on a mission to prove a point. Garrett is the drummer for Beckoning Reality. He's not anyone she should get involved with, but I watch as she strolls up to him. He raises his arms out to greet her, only she doesn't back out of his hold. When she remains flush against him, he looks at her with surprise and a shit eating grin that I could knock straight off his face.

I leave the stage area with one thing on my mind—Lilly. *Damn, I need a drink.* Eaven meets me in the hall with her hand on her hip. I don't need to hear her shit right now. This whole thing is fucked up and the worst part is that I'm letting her get to me. It's not like I want to be exclusive with anyone, but does she really have to rub up on that asshole?

"Luke, did you really just fuck a skank in the bathroom?" I'm honest. She asks, I have to tell her.

"Sure did."

"Was she worth it?" Her pissed off behavior is frustrating me.

"Really, Ev? It's not anything new that I hook up with a girl before a concert. Why is it a big deal today?"

"Because you should've seen her face when you closed the door."

"Yeah, well we aren't exclusive and she knows that. Hell, in fact *she's* the one that made that statement. Not sure what you want from me. I'm not going to stop living it up because you don't approve, Ev. You'll just have to get over it. Just because everyone else here is married and settled, doesn't mean the rest of us have to act that way."

I walk away from her before she makes me any madder at myself. *How many times can I fuck up?* There's a reason she was off limits, and all of these people being in my business is becoming the obvious main reason. Unfortunately, she's worth anything they throw at me.

I think it's time for a night out on the town. I invite all of the guys out to club Kenza in hopes of having a good time and burying the hatchet. Talon and Taron decide to come along with most of the security team. 'Deception' will be playing and I've heard some decent things about them. It's always good to build up a network out on the road anyway. A few of the guys from 'Beckoning Reality' decide to come with us.

This place is packed and my eyes are quick to find a couple of hot girls wondering around the club. Maybe I can convince them to *both* take care of me tonight.

I meet Phoenix real quick. He introduces me to some guy named Reece, who seems like a real asshole.

"Reece. This is Luke, from 'Rebel Walking'."

"Luke." The dude doesn't have an ounce of social skills. I let my eyes find the two girls I plan to get to know a little better.

"You've spotted my fiancée." Phoenix is very quick to notice me eyeing those two.

"You're not engaged to the both, though. Which one's yours?" I rub my chin and hope he tells me the girl with the lighter hair is up for the taking.

"The dark haired one. Thalia. The other one is her best friend, Callie... she has a thing for you." *Oh, this can't get any better. I need to meet this girl.*

"I think I'll go say hi then. She has gorgeous legs and a tight ass."

"You have no idea," Reece finally speaks. I have a feeling this guy thinks he has a claim to this Callie girl by his reaction, but I wasn't given the hands off so it's a go.

I work through the crowd with this girl in my direct line of sight. She's cute and I could use a distraction right now.

I introduce myself to her and work my way into touching her curly hair. "Your hair is so soft. I bet a gorgeous girl like you gets that a lot." *What a lame pickup line.* I need to bring my game and I'm talking about soft hair. She's very shy, almost too timid for me.

"Only once before." She seems to struggle with something before she begins to run a finger along my arm.

"So tell me, Luke.... are you really known as the panty stealer?" She's starting to act slightly braver and it cracks me up to watch when girls fight their inner self to be bold in situations like this. She cocks an eyebrow waiting for my answer.

"That's actally Taron—or was—but tell me, are you going to let me steal *yours*?" I return her gesture and slide a finger up her arm sending chills over her skin.

She leans in close to my chest, ready to whisper in my ear, "To steal mine, I'd have to be wearing them."

That's it. I pull her close with my hands on her hips.

"Luke, get your ass over here." Taron is trying to cock block me again.

"Taron, cut the shit. I'll be there in a minute." I turn my attention back to Callie, "You staying around? We can get some drinks later, here at the club."

"Okay. I'd like that," she says through a smile.

"I'll be back real soon." Backing away from her, I almost fall on my ass by tripping on some fucking cord that isn't properly laid.

We move to a table and start to order a round of drinks. The guys start to give me hell about trying to hook up with Callie so quickly.

"You guys remember how it is. It doesn't take long to get one to drop their panties for ya when you look like this."

The twins don't seem as impressed with that statement as the guys from 'Beckoning Reality' do. I know I could have some new partners in crime if I ever need any with these guys.

After a few drinks, I notice her again. I move in for some more conversation, but find her very willing to do more. She pulls me into the hallway, and I'm not feeling like telling her 'no' at this moment, so I run with it.

I start to slide my hands up her soft legs and under that short skirt. She shifts so that my leg fits between hers and she starts to grind against the denim covering my leg. She lays her head back after a few rotations of her hip, exhaling with an appreciative breathy sound. I lean in to kiss her neck just as the brute barrels in to throw her over his shoulder and take her away like a fucking caveman.

"Stay away from her," is all I can make out of his pissed off grumble before he takes her out of sight. She doesn't seem willing to go with him, but I can tell they have something festering between them. It makes me wonder if she was doing all of that out of spite. I'm not worried, though. No harm done in a little innocent playing around.

The night gets pretty crazy and I decide to stay out after Talon and Taron leave. The Beckoning guys continue drinking with me and we walk back to their bus.

When we first get there, they start to harass Garrett through the closed door about whoever his nightly bag is. I really hope it's not Lilly, but I have a gut feeling it is.

They give me the couch to crash on, but for some odd reason I can't sleep for shit.

Chapter Seven

Lilly

Luke disappeared after the show. I'm spending my evening on the arm of Garrett as he greets some of his fans. Most of them want my autograph, too, and he doesn't seem to be bothered with it. When his fans dissolve, he pulls me in close to his side.

"Are you using me, little darlin'?" The shock on my face as he accuses me of what I'm most likely doing has to amuse him. His laughter fills the area and I bow my head in shame.

"Don't worry about it. It's really not a burden to have you rubbing all over me to prove a point. I think I could get used to it, if you want to make a habit of it."

"Garrett, it's not like that. I'm just hanging out with you tonight and having some fun. Can't a girl have a little fun?"

"Most girls can. Can you?"

"You have no idea." I lead him down the hall, trying to consider the best place to prove my point. He pulls back, stopping our progress all together.

"If I get to have a piece of you, it's not going to be in some fucking bathroom. Come to my bus and I'll let you show me this good time you're talking about."

He leads me to the bus and I follow him to the back where the small bedroom is. I don't even want to know how many skanks he's bagged on that bed. He tosses his jacket on the floor and prowls toward me like a hungry animal ready to mutilate its prey. I cringe at his approach and he comes to a dead stop.

"I knew you weren't really in to me."

"When you look at me like that, it's weird. What do you expect?"

"That's my sexy look."

"You should keep working on that."

"Haha. Aren't you the funny one? I have no problem picking up babes every night."

"I'm sure they are *begging* to climb into your bed of love."

"Actually, most of the time we don't even make it onto the bus." He moves to sit on the edge of the bed and I sit next to him.

"I know you have girls begging to get with you. I'm just not that girl. I know you'd be a riot in the sack. I just need a minute to think about some things." Why am I letting Luke ruin any fun I could have? He had no problem hooking up with a chick and practically flaunted it in my face in the process. I deserve to have some fun, too.

I knew this morning, when he was about to leave my room, that nothing would ever be the same again. So much for a casual hook up. Someone forgot to tell my heart not to get attached, but it's been caught for months. Luke is easy to fall for. *Is it bad that I'm thinking about Luke when I'm here with Garrett?*

"So, how hard is it to get back on the road after all of that time off?" His question pulls me out of my thoughts about Luke.

"Oh. It's not too bad. We've been preparing and working hard on the new album, so it really wasn't time off."

"I actually thought of bringing you into some of our concerts. We could've used another kick-ass guitarist on stage."

"That would've been strange. I can't imagine playing without my guys."

"You should do a crossover at one of the concerts. You and I could duel it out rock and roll style."

"What, you on the drums and me on guitar?"

"Hell no. I'd match you on guitar. You think you could match me on the drums?"

"That's something I know I couldn't come close to doing, but name the time and place and I'll show you up on my strings."

"Okay. The next concert. We'll do it in the middle of Beckoning's show." I look up to see the smirk on his face.

"You seem awful smug about this."

"Nah. I just want you on my stage, since I can't have you in my bed."

"I didn't say no. I just said I need some time."

"Fair enough."

We talk for hours about nothing and everything. I learn a lot about what makes those wheels turn in his head. He listens to me as I talk about my childhood all the way up until today. I don't even bother to look at my cell phone, knowing it'll have messages and missed calls out the ass. We don't leave until tomorrow night, so there is no reason I have to check in with the guys.

I end up falling asleep on his bed. He doesn't push me into anything, and it's nice to know he's completely different than I have him pegged. Waking up in the night, I reach for my phone to see what I've missed. Everyone has called me, except the one person I had hoped would. Not even a message from him. This bothers me.

I scoot over in the bed until my back hits solid, naked muscle. Well, at least his torso is naked. I'm actually surprised with Garrett that he's not fully undressed. He wraps his arms around me and we spoon until I fall back to sleep.

We wake to the sound of drunken laughter and loud talking. The rest of his crew stumbles onto the bus and I say a silent prayer that none of them try to come in here and get repulsive.

"Hey, Riggins.... you gonna share again tonight?"

"Fuck off." His voice echoes through my ears because of how close we are. I'm glad I didn't have to deal with all of the other guys tonight. Him protecting me shows a softer side to Riggins than I'm used to.

"You asleep?" This time his voice is a grumbly whisper.

"No."

"I'm horny as fuck with you up against me, so don't move anymore unless you want me to roll you over and show you what I want."

In this moment, it doesn't sound so bad to let him show me a good time. He's extremely hot and just my type. I choose not to move a muscle, knowing that I'm not truly here with Garrett in my mind.

I finally doze back off in hopes of getting some actual sleep this time.

Garrett's alarm interrupts my sleeping. He reaches for it, shuts it off, and begins stretching. I sit up and do the same.

"I better get back to my guys." I look through my messages and missed calls and there's still nothing from him. Is it too much to ask that he be concerned about me? Even as a friend he should be checking on me.

"Yeah. I'm sure they're missing you by now."

"They'll get over it." He watches me move from the bed to slip my shoes on.

"Let me walk you out, I think your bus is nearby." He grabs my hand and pulls me up against his body. Our mouths touch and I wait for him to do something. He doesn't.

"Next time this will go a little differently." I nod, knowing exactly what he means. He turns to walk us out of the room. The bus is littered with bodies of sleeping drunks. I step over a few arms and legs to get to the door before I see him sitting on the couch. I can't explain the look on his face. Is he mad, or sad? Or maybe disgusted?

Garrett pulls me close and places a goodbye kiss on my lips. I'm pretty sure it's for show. It doesn't take a rocket scientist to feel the tension in the room.

We step out of the bus and Garrett leads me in the direction of our home on wheels. I did nothing wrong, yet this feels like a walk of shame if I ever felt one. The way Luke looked at me just now is stuck in my head. *Why should he care what I'm doing?*

Luke

What a fucking fiasco. I knew she was with him. I'm not sure why she felt the need to run to that asshole's bed. I may be with a lot of different girls, but at least I know how to show them respect. He's a fucker, and I wouldn't want my *worst* stalking fan to hook up with him. I have to get through to her.

Jumping up from this alcohol infested couch, I move for the door. Garrett opens it just as I reach for the latch.

"Leaving so soon?"

"Don't fucking worry about me."

"Oh, I promise ya, you're the last thing on my mind." I stop to take in his smile. The urge to punch him straight in the face is disrupted by Lilly's voice.

"Hey. I forgot to grab my jacket. Can you get it for me, Garrett?" He steps into the bus and disappears, leaving me and Lilly there to stare at each other. My hung over state isn't making things any better, but I can't seem to read her right now. She seems mad at me. *What the fuck have I done wrong?*

"Don't you dare, Luke."

"Don't what, Lilly? Don't tell you that you deserve better than to be a notch on that asshole's drum sticks?"

"Fuck you. You're no better...." She stops talking when Garrett opens the door to toss her jacket at her.

"Call me later, Lils." She nods as she turns to walk away from the situation. I follow on her heels, ready to finish this conversation.

"I'm no better than what? Tell me you think I'm like that asshole."

"Just leave me alone, Luke."

"Is that what you really want?" Her steps come to a halt, but she doesn't turn to look at me.

"What I *really* want doesn't matter." She begins to walk again, but I don't follow her. *What a fucked up mess.* This is what I get for crossing that line with her. Our friendship is now a mess and it feels like we are both in self destruct mode.

I choose to give her the space she seems to need and I begin to walk. There's a gym nearby and I could really use the release.

Two hours of lifting doesn't make me feel much better about the Lilly situation. I'm going to have to talk to her today.

Climbing back on the bus, I notice she's the only one anywhere to be seen. I'm sure the others are still in the hotel rooms. I walk up to where she's laying and watch her try to act like I'm not standing here.

"What do you want, Luke?"

"So, you're just going to hop from bed to bed now?" My question sends her upright in an instant and her expression is that of someone who is ready to attack. She's pissed, and so am I, so this is liable to be one hell of an explosion.

"You." She stands and points her finger at my chest, jabbing it to make a point.

"You. Have no fucking right to talk to me like that. You fuck skanks in bathrooms. I don't have to answer to you, just like you don't have to answer to me. Remember, Luke? No. Fucking. Strings. Attached."

"I remember, but you hate that asshole just as much as I do and then you sleep with him after he sniffs you one fucking time."

"Sniffs me? Look. You've got to stop. I don't owe you any explanation and you don't owe me anything. This wasn't supposed to get complicated and you're making it that way."

"You're right. I *can* and *will* fuck anyone I want without your approval. I just don't want to see you turn into a fucking loose bitch willing to open her legs for anyone."

"I opened them for you, so I guess it's a little late for that." Her words hit home. She thinks I'm just anyone. Point made very clear. This has turned into chaos and I don't know how to fix it.

"I'm sorry I said anything. You can do whatever you want. I have no right to say anything or try to talk you out of anything." Her eyes fall to the floor while she tries to comprehend my apology. I need her to work this out with me and not fight me on everything during this tour. The Walkers will for sure have my ass if that happens.

"Thank you. Sorry I laid into you so harshly. We just need to keep things on a friend level, because we obviously have problems taking it beyond that." Her words are only slightly louder than a whisper.

I want to disagree with her, but after the last twenty-four drama packed hours, I have to agree.

Chapter Eight

Lilly

I should've probably clarified to Luke that I didn't 'sleep' with Garrett, but it really is none of his business. I wish it was, but it's not. He made that clear yesterday.

He stays on board the bus with me, and it's really an awkward attempt at a conversation. I wish I could turn back time and never go there with him, but damn it was so good. I'll probably always have him in the back of my head when I'm out with other guys, but it's obvious that he's nowhere near ready to settle down to one girl. He needs to live it up while he's young and becoming famous.

"Come eat some lunch with me." He stands and pulls my hand toward the door.

"I'm good."

"No. Come with me. I need to find food and this will be good for us to do something like we used to do." How do you tell Luke Jacobs no? I've yet to figure this out, so I rise up from my sitting position and walk behind the six foot solid muscle of man.

He leads me down the street to a small mom and pop cafe. I watch him practically inhale his food and try to enjoy his conversation.

"So what do you think about releasing our song at the next venue?" He surprises me with this. We wrote a couple of songs, but we weren't going to release this one until we felt it was perfect.

"I thought we were going to work on it some more."

"Eh. I think it's perfect the way it is. It's rough around the edges, but so are we. Taron and Talon will nail it and it'll be epic." The excitement on his face reminds me why I love chilling with him so often. He loves what he does. His passion shines through in his performance and I share that same love of music. This is why we usually get along great.

"Yeah. I guess you're right. Let's run through it during warm-up and then release it during the next show."

His playful personality starts to shine through again. It's important that we reach that level of comfort we once had. We'll be spending so many days together in the next few weeks, and I can't have the insanity that we've been dealing with while I'm trying to focus on our performance at each of these venues.

My phone vibrates and I look to see that Garrett is sending me messages. That's funny, because I didn't give him my number, yet my phone says 'Garrett' on the message header.

Garrett: Hey, babe. Looking forward to playing against you at the next show.

I look up at Luke and choose to put my phone in my pocket until I have time to concentrate on the text. He seems to notice a change in me, but thankfully doesn't say anything about it. The rest of our time out is spent just shooting the bull and talking about every day things. Nothing specific or earth shattering happens.

We move back to the bus when the rest of the crew messages us that it's time to load up for the short trip to the show. I need a shower and this isn't a good situation to go into right before a concert.

"Shit. I need to shower and clean up before tonight."

"I'll tell them we'll meet them there. Grab your stuff and come with me." He starts to make a few phone calls and reservations at a hotel.

"We both need to shower, so I just got us a cheap room so we can clean up. I told Taron that we'd meet them there before it's time to go on stage." This is *not* a good idea, but I have no choice.

We arrive at the hotel and he checks us in. He opens the door to let me pass through first. I take note of the kingsized bed and how comfortable it looks, but quickly take the bathroom. My hair and makeup will take longer than his shower.

He didn't say anything the whole way up the three flights to our room. This is a little awkward, but I'm trying to work past it. I need to let my feelings for him go. I just can't stand that I'm attracted to him like this. Too bad it's not a switch I can turn off and on when needed.

The shower feels so nice, and I try to rush so he has plenty of time in here, too. Wrapping a towel around myself and another around my hair, I step out of the bathroom. He's immediately watching me as I stroll past him. I begin to rub lotion on my legs and attempt to act as nonchalant as possible.

I watch him watching me before he walks into the bathroom. Knowing that sexy beast is naked in the next room does something to me. I just wish we were at the same place right now in life, but we aren't even close.

I slide on my painted-on skirt and cleavage-baring shirt to get ready for tonight's concert. Grabbing my blow dryer and flat iron, I take over the small desk in the room. The mirror above it works in my favor and makes it easy to put on my makeup.

I hear the water shut off and shortly after the door to the bathroom opens. A flash of naked skin catches my eye, so I turn to see what he's doing.

"Is there a reason that you're butt-ass naked?" He's drying off, but he's moving the towel around so that I can see everything.

"I'm just drying off. Do you have a problem with the way I dry off?"

"Really, Luke?"

"What? I was just reacting to your show!"

"My show? I was just putting lotion on." *Shit, he saw right through my intentions.* I should've known he would.

"Right.... and I'm just drying off!"

I turn to finish my hair, but the urge to turn and watch his gorgeous body while I have the chance is killing me. A girl should be able to look and enjoy some eye candy when it's offered up in front of her. At this rate, if I look over there, it's likely that I'll make us late to the concert.

I should still be mad at him, but he has lifted my anger and somehow made me crave him again.

That is so fucking not fair that I can hardly stand it.

Luke

Pestering her is what I do best. This is why we've become such great friends. I love to see the smile on her face, and when I act crazy she can't hide her emotions. Her laugh is very seldom heard, but awesome if you get the chance to experience it.

I finish drying off and get dressed in record time. She's still primping when I finish, so I lie across the bed and begin scrolling through my phone. There are six girls messaging me right now, trying to either hook up or talk about when we can get together to hook up. Some of these girls don't mess around with formalities.

I probably get twenty nude pictures a day from different girls trying to catch my eye. I'm not going to lie, some get my attention. I'm a guy and I obviously enjoy a good time. Lilly has never sent me a picture. Her picture is in my head, and that's where it needs to stay.

We leave the hotel in search of a cab to take us to the venue. After a couple of them pass us by, one finally stops. Our drive isn't too bad, and if it wasn't for traffic it would've only been a few minutes long.

I get the evil eye from the guys when we arrive. I'm sure they think the worst of me right now, but I can handle it. Getting their approval isn't really a concern of mine, especially since Lilly and I aren't exactly trying to become a couple.

Our warm-up sounds stiff and unconnected. Lilly notices it, too, and puts all of us in our place. She starts by nailing Talon to the wall.

"Talon, let the shit go. We need to be at our best and we can't do that if half of us are pissed at the other half. Fucking get over it. I'm a grown woman who is capable of taking care of herself. I don't need you guys fighting my battles. As a matter of fact, I don't have any battles to fight, except with you right now. So get the fuck over yourselves."

"Lilly, you know we just want what's best for you. You deserve to be treated right and that's all we want."

"Yeah, well, what I want is a guy that's not afraid to grab me by the hair and fuck me hard, so at least *one* of us wins." She turns and walks out of the small room. The looks on Talon and Taron's faces are priceless. My laughter escapes even though I try to hold it in. If I'm not mistaken, this is their first glimpse of the sex kitten that I have recently met.

Neither of them says another word. Their shock and awkward expressions last a few minutes before we break the ice again. She might be trying to kill me or get me killed, but I have to love the fact that she just handled these guys. It's a very difficult job silencing these two, especially Taron.

She returns to the room and we finally begin to work as a group again. Our sound is near perfect and it almost feels like we're back to one hundred percent. Talon grabs her in for a hug before we leave. I can't hear what he says, but I can only assume he apologizes to her because of her reaction.

Our concert goes as planned and it seems like everything is back to normal. We decide not to encore Lilly's song tonight. We'll take time to fine tune it on the road and reveal it in one of the concerts coming up.

After we move backstage, I notice Lilly talking to Garrett again. She seems to be in to the conversation. I shouldn't let him get to me, but the asshole does.

Walking up to them, I notice him staring me down. It doesn't stop me from continuing.

"Yeah, so the fourth number will be ours?"

"Yes. I'll bring you in from the right side, so stand over there until I bring you on." He walks off and she turns toward me but doesn't look me in the face.

"So, what has *he* cooked up?"

"Luke, he's just using me for one of their numbers in a duel type performance."

"Drums versus guitar?"

"Nah. He's goin' up against me on guitar. I'm not worried about him. I've got this." Her confidence is well-deserved. I know just how good she is—after all, this is something we do all the time. This time she's going to take on another musician on his own stage. If that isn't badass, I don't know what is.

I've seen Garrett on the guitar. He's good, but she will have no problem keeping up with him. A couple of my groupies stand close as I wait for her to go on. The two of them tuck themselves in close to my sides.

I watch proudly as our girl steals the spotlight on stage with 'Beckoning Reality'. She has fun with it and isn't afraid to tear it up. They treat her with respect and they get the reaction they deserve. The crowd goes wild in response to this never before seen performance.

She seems comfortable with Garrett, almost as secure as she is with me on stage. Don't get me wrong, I'm happy to see her succeed, I'd just like to be a part of her success.

The lights go out and I wait for her to exit. She goes the other direction, so I begin to move around the back to find her. With the groupies on my heels, I see her step down into a group of fans. Her smile is captivating and she's obviously loving this moment with her fans.

I stand back and watch until a guy begins to grope her. Holden and the guys are nearby and move in quickly, but the whole thing hits me wrong. Storming through the crowd, I push my way until I reach this motherfucker. He's cocky and obviously drunk as he stutters and starts to sway a little. I hold him up by his shirt and pull his face right into mine.

"Hands off of her, motherfucker."

"Ahh. She likes it. I'm sure she's a slut, dressed like that." There's no need for any other words. My grip on his shirt switches to his neck and quickly turns lethal. Slamming him into the nearby wall becomes my one and only mission. I want this fucker to shut his mouth. Pushing through the fans again, I'm abruptly pulled to a stop. Holden and Aiden both have my shoulders and both begin to pull him out of my grip.

"He's not worth it, man. Let it go." I let Holden's words sink in. If I assault this motherfucker like I want to, there'll definitely be controversy. The last thing 'Rebel Walking' needs is any more publicity. Thinking hard about all of the consequences, I release my grip of this bastard. Aiden pulls him away and Holden stays to pull me out of the crowd.

The fans part like the Red Sea when I begin to walk through. The anger in my eyes and the pissed off look on my face probably has them all concerned for their own lives. That fucker set me so far off. *Who does he think he is touching her like that and acting like he has the right to it?*

Searching for Lilly, I shove off Holden's hold on me. I don't see her anywhere and it's frustrating the hell out of me.

"Where is she?"

"She's back on stage near Garrett. He stopped playing the drums to pull her back on and away from all of this."

"What the fuck, Holden. Tighten security before I kick your ass."

"Chill. We had it under control. You just need to calm the fuck down."

"I'll calm down when that asshole is out of my sight and I know she's okay."

"Follow me to the other side and you'll be able to see her."

Walking back around, I try to take a few deep breaths to calm my shit. It pisses me off how quickly that set me off, but he deserved what I wanted to do to him. He needs to show some damn respect.

Chapter Nine

Lilly

What the hell just happened? I swear shit gets out of control so quickly around here. Watching Garrett strike through his solo on the drums is actually pretty hot. Drummers always captivate me when they really get into it, especially when they're built like he is.

I'm positioned near the stage, but toward the back like I'm Garrett's exclusive fan. It's like a front row to him only on the sideline.

Glancing across stage, I see Luke watching me. His expression is chaotic and concerned. I'm not sure what his deal is, but he needs to quit getting mad at me for talking to Garrett. He's made it very clear that we aren't exclusive or even going to hook up any more at this point.

Garrett just protected me from the crazy fans, so I can stand here and enjoy the show without feeling guilty. I'll deal with Luke later.

Their show ends with a bang and that last piece was badass. As I wait for the lights to come back on, I'm pulled behind the curtain with a determined tug. When we come to a stop, I feel Garrett up against me. His breath blows over my face, almost like he's out of air from exertion.

He pulls my face toward his and lays a kiss on my lips. I hesitate briefly, but then join in when his tongue brushes over my lips. We share a long kiss, wrapped up in a black curtain that shields us from being seen.

It's soft and sensual, *so* unlike how I expected a kiss from him to be. It goes on for a while before he pulls away.

"You are so damn sexy. It should be illegal for you to look like you do. I want a chance with you." My laughter probably could have been timed a little better, but I can't help it. This is Garrett talking to me like this.

"What are you laughing at? I should get a chance to show you the real me." I know he isn't all bad. He's proven he has somewhat of a nice bone in his body, but this is Garrett.

"Okay. What do you have in mind?"

"Travel with me to the next venue. Spend time with me on the bus and we'll get to know each other. Then I'll take you to dinner or something when we get a chance. Let's just be real with each other."

His request isn't out of line. It's actually appealing to have a change of scenery for a long drive.

"Okay. I can handle that." We move from our little space in the corner and walk back to the rest of his band. He's holding my hand as we walk right in the path of Luke.

"Lilly, are you good?"

"Yeah. I'm good."

"I saw that asshole try to grope you."

"Yeah. It's no biggie. Garrett pulled me back into safety. Thanks, though." His eyes move over my hand inside of Garrett's, but he doesn't say anything or act like it bothers him. I know where I stand with Luke, but that doesn't mean I can't wish he felt differently.

Everyone scatters different ways after the crowd thins out. Luke is nearby, but the rest of them are nowhere to be seen. I appreciate the slow tour schedule so we have time to breathe between venues. The last tour was ridiculously non stop. There weren't very many nights in the hotel on that tour, but this time it helps that we have a baby going along with us.

I wonder how long they'll bring Heaven on tour with us. I know the grandmas plan to come get her for the last week of the tour, but other than that she's along for the ride. She's at a good age for this. She sleeps most of the time and we have enough of us that she's kept out of the commotion. There's rarely a time that Taron isn't with her. Actually, he's only away from her when he's on stage.

"You ready to hit the bus with me?"

"Yeah. I just need to grab a few things from my own. Our group isn't leaving until morning."

"We're pulling out tonight."

"Okay. Let me get my stuff while you load up the rest of your gear." I walk over to Luke and see him working on two different girls. He's a huge flirt and he knows it. This works for him, it just sucks to watch from my side.

"Hey. I'm going to ride with Garrett. We're leaving out in the next couple of minutes."

"You sure about that?" He walks toward me, leaving the skanks behind him.

"Yeah. He wants me to and I think it'll be interesting to get to know those guys." He doesn't respond, only nods and begins to walk away.

"Where are you going?"

"I guess to find the others." He's upset—I just don't get his hot and cold behavior all of the time. It's exhausting to be on this side of his emotions.

"What's the problem, Luke?" If he tells me he wants me to go with him, I will in a second. All I need to hear is one single expression that he wants to spend time with me and I'll drop all of my plans for this man.

He pauses in thought, but responds just like I knew he would. "There's no problem, just be careful."

Disappointment has to spread across my face, because it flows through my body in record time. I turn to walk to our bus to get my bag, and then remember I left it in the hotel room before the show.

"Shit. I left my bag in your room."

"Do you have time to go get it?"

"I'll have to make time. It's the one bag I have to take with me."

"I'll go with you to get it."

"Let me tell Garrett what's going on."

Walking over to tell Garrett, I notice the skanks lurking in the shadows again. These bitches just don't know when to stop. Don't they have any fucking morals? I guess they don't if they're prepared to just stand by and be the doormat to all of these guys.

I need to work on getting myself a group of guys just waiting on me to snap my finger before they fall to their knees for me. That shit is just ridiculous and disgusting, but it's how it goes. These girls just want a minute of time with these guys, just so they can tell everyone they did the deed with a rock star.

"Hey. I left my bag at the hotel. I'll have to go get it." He pulls away from the group to address me.

"You want me to go with you?"

"I'll get it. Just text me when you're done here and maybe you can swing by to get me."

"Sounds good." He raises his eyes to Luke over my shoulder and pulls me in for another kiss. This one is rough, just like he's marking his territory right here in front of everyone. It almost pisses me off, until he ends it softer, reminding me of our previous encounter.

I leave the area knowing Luke will follow me out. This is awkward, and I don't even want to hear him complain about Garrett or start dogging him. It's a known fact that Luke doesn't like Garrett, but he doesn't have to approve of who I see. It would be easier if he did, but it isn't a requirement.

"You really like that bastard, don't you?"

"Ehh. It's Garrett. He's fun to hang out with. I'm not sure anything will ever come of it, but I may as well have some fun in the process." He drops the subject of Garrett and attempts to make small talk while we travel to the hotel. There are a couple of times I'm screaming in my head for him to just ask me to stay with him.

Just ask me to stay. Please. I want that more than anything.

Luke

I can't believe she wants to spend time with him. He's such a pompous ass who disrespects women all the time. I may get around, but I always treat the ladies right. Telling her how I feel again will only cause more problems between us. It's time I leave her alone about him, but I'll be watching closely. If I see a single sign that he disrespects her, I'll rearrange his face.

Our ride to the hotel is quiet. I wish I could say something to make her reevaluate what she's about to do, but she's made it clear what she wants. In the grand scheme of things, it's just a road trip with him. Maybe she'll realize his lack of worth and I'll never have to worry about this again.

"How much time do you have?"

"Not long. I'd like to hurry and shower again if at all possible."

"Yeah. No problem."

When we hit the room, she begins to scurry around for the shower. I stand still and watch her scattered thoughts leave her almost ridiculously giddy about leaving soon.

The sound of the water again reminds me just how close, yet so far away she really is. I could go into the bathroom and push my way into the shower with her. That's exactly what I want to do, but that wouldn't be fair to her. She needs to be able to step out of our circle and have a good time with other guys. It's just not supposed to suck this bad for me.

She turns off the water and I hope she makes another appearance like she did before, but she doesn't. She comes out of the bathroom fully dressed, but to my satisfaction she's wearing a hoodie and sweat pants. This isn't screaming sexy and I'm happy to see that it's how she'll be going to Garrett.

"Just text me when you guys are about an hour from location tomorrow. I'll watch for you and try to get as much of the small stuff out of the way during the day."

"I will, but I'm texting you through the night to make sure you make it okay."

"You don't have to. I'll be with their whole crew."

"Exactly why I'll be checking on you."

"Don't start, Luke." She seems irritated as she checks her phone for the message that just came through.

"They're here. I guess I'll see you tomorrow." I move to open the door for her and watch her walk out of my room. The instant regret of not trying to stop her fucks me over the rest of the night. Choosing not to leave my hotel room is easy. Dealing with the shit going through my head, not so much.

The next day goes by slow as hell. Aiden and a couple of the other guys attempt to brighten my mood with no success. I know I suck to be around, but I really don't give a shit what anyone thinks about me right now. I haven't texted her, trying to give her the privacy she deserves. She should've checked in, but she hasn't. We're almost two hours from location, so I'm trying to hold out until we're closer to text her.

This shit shouldn't be irritating me so hard, but it is.

Damn it.

Chapter Ten

Lilly

He made himself clear. I'm going to enjoy myself with Garrett and the guys. I know this can be a great trip if I let it be.

He's standing outside the bus when I walk out. His greeting doesn't surprise me this time—I could get used to his kisses and show of affection. He's a great kisser, not as good as Luke, but none the less he's great at it. The other guys start to yell obscenities at us, and he pauses to look me in the eye before he turns to nail their asses. His efforts only gain laughter, but it doesn't seem to faze him in the least.

"Did you dress up for me?"

"You like it?"

"You can wear whatever you want with me. I'll just try to get you out of it anyway." He's always the flirt. It feels nice to be wanted like this. He's never hidden his attraction to me, sometimes coming across as an egotistical ass when making his comments.

"Very funny."

"Honey. I'm not joking." I know he's not joking, so I start to step toward the bus to face these grown men that are sure to act like idiots when I open this door.

To my surprise, they don't harass me. They invite me for a shot and make a place for me at the table to play quarters. I've never been great at this game, but I'm willing to give it a shot.

"Ladies first!" Garrett sits down beside me just as the bus begins to roll. A few rounds go by, and so far, I'm not doing too bad. I spread the shots around to each guy when I make the glass, but it isn't long before they all begin to zone in on me. I know it's not a great idea to get trashed in a bus full of guys, no matter how well I know them, so I pull from the game.

"I'm out."

"What? I knew you couldn't hang." Grayson seems to be leading the bash Lilly campaign tonight. I'm sure it's all out of fun, but I can see this quickly turning into a nightmare if I keep this up.

"Yeah. I'm zapped. I need to sleep soon." Garrett runs his hand up my leg, straight for my crotch area. Trying not to cause a scene, I grab his hand to hold in my lap instead.

The guys all continue the game, and within an hour, they're all ridiculous and loud. My stomach hurts because of the laughter from their hysterical reenactments of stories from their past. We stay up until 3:30 in the morning like this.

Garrett finally speaks up about going to bed. He pulls my arm until I follow him into the tiny back room. The feeling is all too familiar and I drop on the bed, taking up the side of the bed I slept on before.

He begins to strip out of his clothes, so I turn to watch him, wondering if he'll go all the way down to nothing. Oh, yeah he does.

He crawls onto the mattress and proceeds until he is over me.

"Do you plan on staying in those sweats all night?" I can't hide the grin on my face. I like his forwardness, but am I really ready for this? What's holding me back? I'm not in an exclusive relationship. Garrett is hot and definitely in to me. Why not have a great night of sex with this man?

I begin to slide the waistband down my legs and pull the shirt over my head. Lying here in my bra and panties is a whole different situation. Now I can feel his eyes scrape over my skin and it's making me feel self-conscious. I know he's been with beautiful women in his time, so I don't need him to see my flaws.

"Turn out the light." He does what I ask and returns, all hands and mouth. He leaves no space on my body untouched and sends me through my orgasm before his own release. I know I shouldn't be comparing the two, but he's no comparison to Luke. I'm going to hell for thinking like this while I'm still in the arms of a man who's trying really hard to make me happy.

Sleeping comes easily and morning shows up way too quickly. I begin to stretch and notice he's not in the bed anymore. I check my phone for messages only to not find a single one. Luke was supposed to check on me, but he hasn't sent any messages. I told him not to start any crap, so I guess this is his way of keeping the peace.

Hearing laughter, I climb off the mattress to get dressed. I see the proof of our time together on the window ledge. Wrapping it up in toilet paper, I toss it in the trash of the tiny bathroom. My face in the mirror disgusts me, so I try to freshen up some. It's nearly impossible to do anything about it while we travel down the road.

I do what I can and then start to open the door. I stop moving when I hear their voices.

"Another notch on your sticks, huh?"

"Yeah. She was a great add to the collection. Hand me that knife."

"Dude, your sticks are full of slice marks. You're gonna have to start a new set soon."

"I'll make room. I have this whole side on this one open." I walk out just as he's running the blade across the wood. *Is it possible to feel any lower about myself than right now?* I'm just another skank to him. This is a huge blow to me, and I'm going to have to figure out how to get through the rest of this day dealing with this asshole. I can't believe I fucking let myself become like this.

I'm worth more than a quick lay.

"Are you really marking me off as one of your skanks?" He turns to look at me with a shitty expression on his face. I can tell this is not going to go well.

"Yeah. What did you think you were? Just another honey, sweet-ass fuck."

"Fuck you, Riggins."

"Nah. Already did that, babe."

"You're an asshole."

"Never said I wasn't"

"Where the fuck are we?"

"Between there and here somewhere."

"Stop the fucking bus."

"Chill out, babe. You really need to calm the fuck down."

"Stop the fucking bus before I make your fucking life hell."

"You really want to be dropped off in the middle of nowhere?"

"I'd rather be *anywhere* than with your ass. Fucking stop the bus, NOW."

He tells the driver to pull over and I don't waste any time stepping off the bus. I use my phone to locate where I am and begin to walk. Luckily, I'm only a mile from a small town. I should call the guys, but there's no way I want them to know what I've done.

I really deserve this. If you act like a ho, you can't get mad when you're treated like one. This feeling of filth is horrible. I'll never let this happen again.

Is it too much to ask to be important to someone? Why does it seem they all just want sex with no emotion? I need to feel connected and this isn't working out for me.

The mile walk isn't too bad. I'm thankful that I chose to wear my tennis shoes and not any of my heels. That would have been torture.

I walk into a convenience store and purchase a water. They have booths and a small diner, so I take a seat. I figure it's time to sort my thoughts out and get a plan.

I'm about thirty miles from the venue. I have eight hours to kill and the crew won't be rolling into town for hours. Using my phone to search the internet, I find a car rental place not too far down the road. I call them to make sure they have a car available before I start to walk again. This walk is another two miles, but I welcome the time to think about things.

I'm really glad it's daylight and no one bothers me during my walk. *What have I become?* Is this really me, stranded in a strange town after just having meaningless sex with yet another rock star?

I take the car and begin to drive down the long, lonely highway. My thoughts consume me and I just keep driving. We have a break for four days coming up next week. Maybe I should take a break from everything and everyone during that time. I never want to let the guys down no matter how badly I want to skip out. We've worked so hard to get to this point.

I'm just bass guitar, they can do the show without me, but it wouldn't be complete. I decide to message Luke and tell him that I'm in the middle of nowhere. It's not safe for me to be out here like this and no one know where I am.

Lilly: You were right.

Luke: What happened?

Lilly: He's an asshole.

Luke: Are you ok?

Lilly: Yeah. I'm renting a car so I can get there tonight.

Luke: Where the fuck are you?

Lilly: A town named Henderson. I'm ok. I'll see you there tonight.

Luke: Damn it. From now on you stay with us. I'm going to kick his ass for letting you out of the bus.

Lilly: He didn't have a choice.

Luke: What the hell did he do to you?

Lilly: Nothing I didn't deserve.

Luke: This convo isn't over. I want to know how bad I'm going to beat his stupid ass.

Lilly: Luke, it's no big deal. I had it coming. It was just a blow to my ego. I was just another notch on his drum stick and it just hit me wrong. I had it coming.

His reply doesn't come for a while. It seems like he's forgotten about me, it takes him so long to come back with a message.

Luke: You deserve better.

Chapter Eleven

Luke

I'm losing my fucking mind right now. How the fuck can she just message saying she got off a bus in the middle of nowhere? I should've stopped her from going last night. Why the fuck I didn't, I'll never know. I message Garrett to see what the hell happened, with no response.

I'll *kill* his ass if he hurt her.

Holden tries to locate her and says she's in a small town named Henderson. She is obviously hours ahead of us and this will be a long-ass day of traveling and worrying about her.

I continue to text her throughout the day to check on her. She found a shopping mall and killed some hours there until we could pull into the parking lot to meet up with her. There was a rental car place nearby that we followed her to so she could drop off her car.

The tension was very high with all of us until we could see for ourselves that she made it alright. There hasn't been a second that's gone by today that I haven't wished I had made more of an ass of myself to keep her at the hotel last night. I really feel like it still would've drove her to him, and then she wouldn't have felt like she could turn to me when he dumped her.

She steps onto the bus and everyone starts in on her. They all want to know the how, when, and where. The only thing that seems to be understood is the who before she begins to tell us all to drop it.

"What the hell, guys? It's all good. Yes, he's an asshole, but this is what happens when you go to bed with an asshole." I watch as the twins cringe from her words.

"You fucked Riggins. Shit, Lilly. This is out of control." Talon turns to walk toward the back of the bus. I can tell this is more than he really wants to know.

"You need to be more careful with these guys, Lilly. Unfortunately, most of them want only one thing." Holden tries a softer approach.

"I know men are scum. I'm not a young innocent thing myself. I just refuse to be treated like that." I can tell she's humiliated about everyone knowing her business. Staying out of the conversation, I make myself as scarce as you can in a bus full of people.

When it all calms down a bit, we begin to move again. This time, I have something to handle the second the wheels stop moving. Garrett will be there and I plan to deal with his ass directly.

We pull onto location and every one of us barrels off the bus to find that asshole. Garrett's smug ass is laid back with his arm over the back of the couch when we bust through the door.

"Who the fuck do you think you are, dropping her off on the side of the road?"

"She wanted off the bus some forty-five miles back. Calm the fuck down." There are four men charging his ass at once—he doesn't stand a chance. We all fight our way to him and Holden yanks him up with hardly any effort. The other members of Beckoning choose not to fuck with us.

"You're fucking lucky that she isn't hurt. I would gut your ass in a second. Do you understand me?" Holden's no nonsense demand mirrors my own thoughts. The rage in his voice matches the craze in his eyes.

"Let go of me or I'll be pressing assault charges on you." Holden adds an extra shove when he uncurls his fingers from the grip he has on Garrett. We all storm out of the room and begin to pace the floor.

I've never seen Holden this mad. We're all infuriated.

"She's safe. We have to trust in that and let her have her space." Eaven moves through the room, headed straight for Talon.

"What's our plan for tonight's show?" This time it's Aiden who speaks up, probably trying to calm everyone down.

"We go on as scheduled," Talon says, looking in to Eaven's eyes. I hate this. I could've stopped all of this by tying her to the bed and holding her hostage. All of that sounds better than what we're dealing with right now.

The show isn't our greatest to date. The tension between us and the guys of 'Beckoning Reality' proves to be too much for us to get past in such a short amount of time.

We have to somehow learn to deal with those bastards because this tour is full of piggyback nights with them. That asshole doesn't deserve to be near her, but we can't do a damn thing to stop it except threaten him.

He's cocky and seems to thrive on pissing her off. The way he's talking to her like she's a piece of trash one minute and then acting completely opposite the next has Lilly on edge.

Lilly

This is such a shitty day. I need it to be over, like hours ago. How embarrassing is this crap? I don't need these guys to fight my battles. I just wish they'd all stop with the damsel in distress shit. I'm fine.

It would be nice to take a shower and go to bed. That's all I need right now.

We are the first to go on tonight, so we load up immediately following and get the hell out of there. We check in to another hotel and I welcome the burn of the hot, hot water on my skin. I love how hotel showers never seem to lose hot water. You don't realize how important that is until nights like this.

Stepping out of the shower, I hear a knock on the door. I wrap up in my towel and check the peep hole. Luke is standing there waiting for me to open the door. I contemplate letting him in, but I really just need a night to myself. *Will he be offended if I don't let him in?*

His gorgeous smirk wins me over, so I open the door enough for me to just see him through the crack.

"Hey. What's up?"

"Just checking on you."

"I'm good. You guys need to stop worrying about me. I'm not the fragile little bitch you all have me pegged as."

"I know you're not, but I have the right to check on you."

"Luke, I'm really not in the mood tonight."

"I get that. Just call me if you need anything. I'm in room 322, just down the hall." I watch his face lower in defeat. He's just trying to cheer me up and I'm being a closed off bitch, not even letting him in the door for a few minutes. He begins to walk away, so I step out the door to address him face to face.

"Luke, wait. Come in and keep me company for a little while." As I'm saying this my towel begins to slip, so I hurry to keep it up, letting go of the door in the process. The room keys are inside and here I am, standing naked in the hall, with only a towel to shield me from gawking eyes.

Luke's eyes get wide and he starts to laugh. How could you not laugh? This is an insane way to end this hellacious day. The room is in my name only, therefore I have to go to the front desk for a key to the room. *Shit. This is not happening to me right now.*

"Come to my room. We'll call downstairs to get you a key."

"Wait. Isn't Aiden in your room?"

"Yes, but your other option is to stand out here in the hall to see which Walker comes out to see us talking while you're naked." When he says it like that, I look forward to seeing Aiden in that hotel room. I don't want any more drama tonight. *Can't a girl just relax and get some rest?*

I tuck my towel in tighter and start to walk down the hall with as much pride as one can in this situation. He walks fast and I appreciate it. I hear him begin to warn Aiden the second he opens the door.

"Hey, Lilly is locked out of her room.... and she's naked. You need to turn the fuck around and give the girl some privacy,"

"What the hell? I'm not naked. I have a towel covering me."

"Naked enough."

Aiden moves quickly and never tries to show any disrespect as Luke picks up the phone and dials the front desk. His explanation as to why he needs a key to a girl's room doesn't work and they demand that I come down for a new key. He slams the phone down, aggravated, and starts digging in his bag.

"You can put some of my clothes on and go down." He tosses a t-shirt and shorts over. The shorts go past my knees and the t-shirt is big on me, which I'm thankful for since I have no bra on. I go into the bathroom and pull his clothes on.

He insists on escorting me downstairs and sends evil glares at anyone who even *tries* to look my way. Crossing my arms over my chest, I manage to get a new room key and we make it back to the third floor. The elevator opens up and we're faced with Talon and Eaven.

Can this fucking night just end already? They both notice my attire instantly. I'm sure conclusions are drawn and I have to let any cares about it go. It is what it is. Luke and I shouldn't have to answer to anyone.

I hold my head up and step off the elevator. Turning to wave at them both, I say a thankful prayer that they didn't see me in the towel minutes before. Holding on to the shorts as I walk quickly to my room, I get the key ready to enter the slot. I'm going to lock myself in this room and not come out until it's time to pull out of the parking lot.

His footsteps behind me let me know he still wants to come in to talk. I hold the door open long enough for him to enter and then gladly close it for good.

"That did *not* just happen." His laughter verifies his true feelings of the matter.

"Glad *you* think it's funny."

"It is. Something like that would only happen to you."

"Yeah. I know. Fuck my life right now."

"Aww. It's not that bad. It could've been worse."

"How?"

"You could have answered the door completely naked."

"Do you honestly think I'd step into the hall butt-ass naked?"

"*I* would." Slugging him in the arm, I walk over to the bed in the room."

"You totally would."

"Yeah, and I'd stroll my naked ass downstairs to get a new key when they wouldn't work with me over the phone, too." I could see him doing that. I'd die of embarrassment and he'd stand proud. Our laughter and banter continue for hours. It's so nice to have this back. It's only been days since we crossed the line and messed things up, but it seems like a long time when you're used to spending almost every minute of the day with someone.

We both fall asleep in the bed and it's purely innocent the entire night. We needed this and I wake up as happy as I can possibly be.

He doesn't have his shirt on, so I can't help but admire his back when the light starts to shine through the window. Every time I'm this close to him I see a new tattoo that has always been there, but is just now standing out. You could seriously play a game of hidden objects on this man's back. I try not to stir too much and wake him up. Enjoying this moment for as long as I can, I just watch him in silent awe.

Luke

Spending the night with Lilly like this reminds me how much I enjoy her in my daily life. We have a lot in common and she knows everything about me. We don't have any secrets and she just gets me. Our conversation covers everything from more about our sexual history to the fact that she didn't sleep with Garrett that first night.

Talk about regret. I want to rewind time and stop her from leaving with him all over again. I really thought she liked him and was trying to get to know him better. Hearing her side of things is tough, but we make it through it.

I apologize for flaunting my 'skank' in her face and she seems to accept it. Our understanding that we aren't committed to anyone and this is just the beginning of many adventures for both of us seems to come with a sense of relief and concern all in one. It's important that we understand each other; I just hope we can handle it better when it happens again.

I watch her sleep before I doze off. Her crazy bed hair and the fact that she's wearing my hideous clothes should be a turn off, but it's not. I'm not going there with her again anytime soon.

I open my eyes to silence. Rolling over, I catch her looking at me. She tries to avert her eyes before I see her, but she fails. It does something to me to know she was staring at me while I slept. *What's with the two of us creepers?*

"I should probably get back to my room."

"Yeah, probably so." I crawl out of bed at the same time she does. She meets me at the end of the bed and wraps her arms around my waist.

"Thanks for cheering me up last night. I had a great time."

"Anytime. You know I'm here for you."

"So I get to keep the clothes?"

"Uh. If you really want them." Her smile when she pulls back from me is all that I wanted to see when I came here last night. Her happiness means a lot to me and I never want to see her hurt like she has the last few days.

We only have an hour before we need to leave. I want to get some gym time in before we go and I'll need to shower as well. A few of the guys are in the fitness area, so it turns into a pissing contest with the weights. Holden isn't in here, so I kill it against all of those bastards. Holden is the only one who can hang with me in the gym. It goes back and forth with him as to which one of us can lift more. These other guys have the proper form and one day will get there, but my hard work and dedication outweighs all of their efforts any day.

I end up running myself late for a shower, but choose to take one anyway. They should all be thankful that I don't skip the shower just to be on time. We always leave in plenty of time, allowing for extra time for the girls or lil' miss Heaven and any distractions that could happen on a long trip like this.

Today is only a travel day. Knowing that we don't have to go on stage immediately upon arriving is a relief.

I'm the last one on the bus, but it doesn't seem like I've pissed anyone off. Most of them are around the table playing a game of 'Oh hell', and the competitive sounds of laughter blare through the confined space. This game is fast-paced solitaire, and these people get downright nasty when it comes to this game. I watch the girls run circles around Taron and Talon, and decline when they ask me to join.

This drive proves to be exactly like the good old days. There doesn't seem to be stress and we all get to have fun like we usually do. The guys seem to be over being mad at me about Lilly.

Sitting by her most of the day, we encourage each other all day in back and forth teasing; never missing an opportunity to give the other one hell. We don't restrict our aim to just each other, either. There are multiple times we get to let loose on some of the others.

"So, how does it feel to be an old married couple?" Lilly directs her question to Eaven and Talon. They both exchange looks and smile at each other. These two should be on a poster.

" The only real difference is he calls me Mrs. Walker all the time. Everything else is really the same." They've only been married a couple of months, but we all knew it was coming long before then. Just like we know Ivy will eventually say yes to Taron.

Those two girls fell for the twins so hard. I really didn't see Ivy falling for Taron after some of the shit I witnessed between them, but now it's obvious that they are one of those forever stories.

"Yeah, that's about the only difference," Talon agrees and we all start to look at Taron.

"Don't look at me. I've already committed myself to this woman. She's working on getting there. It's all good. I'm not going anywhere, so there's no hurry." Ivy drops her head and places her finger inside Heaven's little grip. I rush to change the subject for her sake. When she's ready, she'll do it. She's Ivy

Adams. You can't make her do anything she doesn't want to do without pure hell to pay.

Chapter Twelve

Lilly

Spending the trip like this is exactly what all of us need. Catching up on life and what all of them went through during our break is interesting. It's also nice to get to know some about the security team. Only two guys are with us, but they offer up a few stories on the others. Those guys are a mess and it's funny to hear all of those stories. They seem so stiff and boring, but these stories prove they are capable of having just as much fun as a rock star.

We arrive at our hotel stop for the night. Some of the guys are talking about going out tonight and Luke is pushing for me to go with them. I'm up for a night out on the town, so I agree. After all, what could go wrong with my own security team surrounding me?

I hurry and dress the part, putting only a little makeup on this time. It's nice to give my face a break from performance night.

Luke knocks on my room door just as I finish and we make our way down to join the guys in the bar of the hotel.

"Well, hi there, Lilly. Are you ready to go out with the guys?"

"Ready as I'll ever be."

Aiden introduces me to all of his crew, "Lilly, you may know some of the guys, but I'll do a run through anyway. This is Drew, Colin, David, and Zander. These guys work day and night to keep you safe."

"Nice to officially meet all of you." Each of them comes forward to shake my hand.

"This isn't all of them, just the ones who want to go out with us. Tonight they're off the clock."

"Let's get going. I'm ready to smash some beers and have some fun." Luke starts to move toward the door.

We step out the doors of the hotel and there's a large SUV waiting for us. Aiden talks with the driver and we all file in. I take the very back and Luke climbs back there with me.

We arrive at the club, and the line outside makes me wish I had worn pants. The chill in the air is going to suck while we stand here. Aiden keeps walking to the front and then finally waves us forward after talking to the bouncer at the door. It's nice having VIP status for once.

This place is massive. I notice the sign at the door says 'Club Volume'. I see where it gets its name right away. The dance floor is full and there's hardly any space around the bar. Luke moves up against the bar and orders us a round of tequila shots and a beer each.

"What are we toasting to?" he asks me and I hate this part. Taron and Ivy usually handle all the toasts. It isn't fun to be put on the spot.

"Um.... To living life, all the way to our last breath." He raises his shot and we take it back.

A kick ass song comes on and I can't resist moving with the music. It's what I do. I take a few drinks of my beer and move to the dance floor. There are a few girls who move in to dance near me and we have a great time dancing through a few songs. A slow song comes on, so I start to walk off the dance floor.

Luke grabs my hand and pulls me back out there. I wish he wouldn't do things like this. It really messes with my head. He's done so good with keeping at a distance lately.

We start to dance and he pulls me in close. Our movement is slower than the song is, but I'm just following his lead.

"You always have to shake that ass of yours, don't you?" I look at him in confusion and try to figure out why he's bringing this up now.

"I was just dancing."

"I know. You're trying to kill me,"

"Sorry."

"Don't be, free bird. I enjoy watching you like that. It's how you are on stage." *Free bird?*

"Did you just call me free bird?" His smile grows when I ask.

"Damn. I wasn't going to ever call you that out loud."

"Why would you call me that?"

"One of my favorite moments is when you and I first played that song together. And besides that, you remind me of a free bird on stage. You should never be caged." I remember the time he's talking about. It was one of the nights at Smitty's before we went on tour the first time. We used to play old music just to get the fans moving. Lynyrd Skynyrd is an easy crowd pleaser.

"I think *you're* the free bird. If you listen to the song, it's you to a tee."

"Maybe so, but it's *your* nickname now." We finish the song before he pulls me to the bar for another shot.

"Your turn this time." I'm going to do my best to avoid having to lead in toasts. The more I drink, the bigger chance I'll say something I shouldn't.

"To never being caged." *Well, if that isn't one hell of a toast.*

We lay it back and I turn to hit the dance floor again. I don't want to stand there and let him see me disappointed in the fact that he never wants to settle down. I wasn't supposed to fall for him. The problem is, I had already begun my descent before I made that promise to myself.

Making it a mission to enjoy myself tonight, I dance with a few guys who ask me. All of them keep it clean and there aren't any issues. The next slow song comes on and I know I need to get off this stage fast. If he tries to dance with me on this one, I'll lose it.

'Say Something' is not the song to try to face him during, especially with how I'm feeling right now.

He moves around to stop my escape and leads me to the edge of the dance floor again. I can't look at him as the words begin to play through the large speakers.

I tuck my head into his chest and let him lead me again. Trying to stop the tears when they won't stop falling becomes impossible. He doesn't say a word during this dance and I turn to walk away as soon as it's over. This song is unbearable and says so many things I want to say to him. *Why would he insist on torturing me through that whole song?*

The line to the bathroom is long, but a few of the women let me pass through quickly. I'm guessing it's the tears running down my face that warrants their kind gesture.

I take the time needed to not look like a complete freak when I walk out of the bathroom. Having an audience while I break down even further isn't a perfect scenario, but I have to work with what I have.

Walking out of the bathroom, I dread seeing him again. I need to get a grip. We are great friends. We'll never be more than that. He's not capable of anything more.

I do my best to stroll up to the bar and ask for another shot with confidence. He meets me and buys us both a drink.

Avoiding the monster in the room is his specialty. He begins to tease me and lightens the conversation to an easygoing feeling. I choose not to dance anymore. We need to eliminate any chances of me acting like a fool again if possible.

As the night goes on, the shots continue to go down. He starts to run his hands over my back and puts his arms around me more than usual. I'm starting to get whip lash from his on and off behavior.

Luke

This night has been one of the strangest yet. I'm having so much fun one minute, the next I've obviously upset Lilly. It seems that we're past whatever it was that had her in tears. I know she's going through a lot right now, but I plan to be here for her when she needs me.

Our drinking has continued and I'm pretty sure we're both completely lit. I wave at Aiden and he starts to round up all the guys.

Aiden has the driver take us back to the hotel and I help her to her room. She's walking on her own just fine, she's just loud and having a lot of fun.

I help her open the door to her room and she grips my shirt with both hands and pulls me into her room. Her mouth crashes into mine and we both begin to tongue battle.

Her desperate tugging on my shirt is awkward since she's shorter than me, so I help her lift it off.

"You're too fucking sexy for your own good." Her boldness makes me laugh. I know she's drunk. This sucks. I can't do this with her after everything we've just been through. If we do this again, I need her to understand where I'm coming from.

I continue to kiss her. This I can do and not feel like a complete jackass in the morning. I need to know that she'd have sex with me sober before I let this happen.

Trying to calm her down long enough to defuse the fire between us both is not an easy task. I turn her around to face away from me long enough to catch my breath and talk to her.

"Let's talk about this in the morning. Tonight I'll just stay with you, to sleep and nothing more." She seems to understand and starts to climb into the bed. I watch her like she's a wild animal that could strike at any moment until she slides under the covers.

I hate sleeping in jeans, but I guess I have no choice. Lying in bed, I remember my shorts she borrowed. Luckily, they're on top of her bag when I open it. I'm pulling them up just as she stands up on the other side of the bed. Her eyes focus right on my dick, and I slide the shorts up quickly to try to salvage my plan to wait.

She lifts her shirt over her head, drops her skirt and panties, then reaches around to drop her bra. In less than ten seconds, she's completely naked. She climbs back in bed and slides under the covers, grabbing her pillow in a cuddle hold like I've never seen before.

I think about this for a second. This is Lilly. We'll always have something special. I can't ruin everything again if I don't know how she feels.

Leaving my shorts on, I slip under the covers and reach to turn off the light. I hold still until I can hear her sleeping.

I feel her slide her hand over my stomach. She's headed into my shorts and I'm ready and waiting for her when she gets there. Sleeping next to this woman is not easy, especially when she's naked. The light from the window tells me it's barely sunrise.

I let her move her hand up and down on my erection, causing my morning wood to grow to capacity. She moves over me to lean off the bed and get a condom from my jeans. I watch her tits in the process and start to grab a hand full of her when I get the chance. She hands the condom to me and rolls onto her stomach.

I'm not jumping straight into this like that. I nudge her to roll back over and crawl between her legs. I need to remind her of what *should* happen before we stick it.

I run my tongue all the way around her clit and don't slow down until she's moaning through an orgasm. Her whimper continues as I do, too. Bringing her up to the point she's going crazy again is easy. This clit piercing is like having a direct line to a quick orgasm.

I pull away before she's able to release again. Moving over her, I rub my cock over her piercing, applying pressure in exactly the right place. In this position, I get to watch her body come undone for me. There's a beauty to watching a female reach an orgasm. Each one is a little different.

I slide inside as she's coming down from the last one. She closes her eyes and rolls her head back as I enter her. *Damn, she's so tight.*

Moving slowly, I make this about pleasing her. I don't rush any of it, and in doing so, it becomes so sensual. This is new to me. It's a strange feeling, but a great one. We're both covered in sweat and exhausted when I finish.

Falling on top of her, I lie there and feel the brush of her fingers over my back, cooling me off with every swipe We lay like that for a couple of minutes before I roll off of her and pull her in to my side.

"We were supposed to talk about this before it happened again." I need to start this conversation with her soon.

"Talking is overrated."

"I need to know that we're good here."

"We are. I love what we have together."

"Me, too."

"Just don't complicate things and we'll take it as it goes. I know we're not exclusive, and you do, too, but that doesn't mean that we have to throw it in each other’s faces if we do anything."

"I agree."

Chapter Thirteen

Lilly

Last night with Luke was incredible. It's hard not to feel more for him than he's willing to give, but I get it. He's not there yet. Maybe time will allow for that, maybe not.

Knowing we have a few days of break after tonight's performance makes me want to make an early trip home. I can see my mom and spend some quality time with her before I have to leave out again. I mention it to Luke and of course he wants to go with me.

He finally gets my drift when I put my foot down that I just want to go home alone. He's not happy about it, but he lets me go.

The drive back to Springfield is long and gives me plenty of time to think about things. I really care about Luke, but he's not ready to be anything more than friends. I can't self destruct during all of this. There's a lot riding on us with the band, and besides that, he has no idea how I feel. It's probably best he doesn't know just how much I care about him.

I finally pull into the driveway of my mom's house. She knew I was coming home tonight and is supposed to be waiting up for me.

She greets me at the door with welcoming arms and a huge hug. I spend hours telling her about our journey and I even tell her what went on with Luke and Garrett. My mom has always been there for me. She knows everything and I know she'd never judge me as harshly as I judge myself.

Her words don't cheer me up, but they make huge strides in me understanding my strengths and weaknesses. I need to find myself before I try to find someone for me. Luke is a great friend, and someone I'll always care about, but beyond that we have nothing at this point. Yes, we crossed the line over friendship and it was fantastic, but our love for each other is a different kind of love. When he settles, it'll be a with different kind of woman—one that yanks him out of his world and leaves him speechless.

It's been two days since I messaged anyone. I need to let everyone know that I'm safe. Telling my mom goodnight, I lock myself in my old room to respond to them.

Lilly: I'm at my mom's. I'm safe.

Luke: Glad you made it ok.

Lilly: I'll see you in two days.

Luke: Definitely.

Falling asleep almost instantly helps me get through the night. I'm exhausted which is obvious when I sleep 'til almost noon the next day.

Luke

We hit Springfield and I just want to see her. I know she said she needs time, but shit, she's had four days to herself. It's time for Luke time. She needs Luke time as much as I need Lilly time. You can't go from spending all that time together to not seeing each other for days upon days.

Tonight is our big bash at Smitty's. She promised to be there for it, but I'm going to go by and get her before I go.

Pulling in to her driveway, I feel relieved. It's time to make sure she's refreshed and ready to hit the rest of the tour. I ring the doorbell and wait.

"Hey, Luke. Come on in. She's upstairs." Lilly's mom is used to seeing me. Our evenings often consist of her inviting both of us over for dinner. I take the steps two at a time until I'm at her door. It's open enough for me to see her doing her hair. I shove through the door and make myself at home on her bed.

"So, you staying at your mom's for a reason?"

"Just wanted to."

"Are you about ready for tonight?"

"Almost."

"Good, because I want to get there in time for a beer or two."

"That sounds good." I watch her finish getting ready. This has become a normal thing, and that should be weird to me, but it's not.

"I'll drive tonight since I'll probably only have one beer." She insists on driving and I let her. Maybe this'll mean that we can go home together after the show. We have some catching up to do.

We arrive at Smitty's to a crowd of people ready to party with us. We always fill this place and it's amazing to come back to where it all began. Smitty helped us get started and we'll always play favorites when it comes to playing here. He wants us monthly, so he gets us monthly.

Talon and Eaven show up right after Taron and Ivy. Our usual table is blocked off just for us, so we gather around to shoot the shit.

"Lilly, if you ever fucking do that again...."

"I know. I know."

"You had us worried." Eaven and Ivy enclose her in a hug together. The bartender brings us a round of beer and it's great that everything is back to normal.

"I just needed some me time. It's no big deal. Where's Miss Heaven tonight?"

"The grandmas are fighting over her," Ivy is quick to respond and Taron busts out in laughter.

"It must be terrible to have so many people who love her." Lilly moves over to talk to the girls, leaving me with the guys. Our group time is cut short by the fans that begin to fill our area.

At home, the fans know Talon and Taron are taken. I usually get all of the attention. Knowing this, I move to sit with

Lilly. I really don't want to deal with anyone tonight. Tonight is all about her.

Before the show, I take the stage for a special announcement. I tap the mic to get everyone's attention. This is a whole different experience, being alone in the spotlight. I feel naked without my guitar strapped over my shoulder.

"Could I have your attention, please?" All the voices in the crowd grow quiet and I proceed to help Ivy with her special message.

"Ivy Adams would you report for duty?" She moves to the stage quickly. It's so great to be able to help her with this.

"Um. Taron Walker, can you please join me?" She pauses while he moves to the stage.

"Please get on your knee. We're doing this right." Taron does just as she asks.

"Taron Walker. I love you. You have proven your love to me over and over. You gave me the best gift in the world and I hope to spend forever with you. It's taken me longer to come to this conclusion than it did you. I love that you have the patience to deal with a woman like me. There aren't many out there who do, but there aren't any others out there that I want to spend my forever with. I have a present for you."

She moves her right hand in front of his face to show off her new tattoo. He grabs her hand and jumps up to lift her off the ground in a hug. He dives in to kiss her and the two of them quickly become a hot public display of affection. He finally carries her offstage and they disappear for some time.

From the look of it, Eaven and I were the only ones who were in on Ivy's secret today. This night quickly turns into an engagement party for another set of Walkers.

We take the stage almost an hour later than scheduled and the show is longer than usual. We decide to encore Lilly's song tonight and it's a huge success. The slow tempo and soft spoken lyrics has everyone falling for it in the first verse. She says we wrote it together, but in all reality she did most of it. I named it and came up with the chorus, but the rest is her doing.

We make a break for the door soon after the show ends.

"Stay the night with me."

"Luke, I can't."

"Not like that. We'll just hang out and catch up. I promise I won't lay a hand on you unless you want me to." I might have just jumped the gun on that last sentence. I plan to have a special night with her and somehow not rush into anything.

Chapter Fourteen

Luke

We both sit in her car and she waits a little bit before starting it. I watch her face light up as I run my hand over her thigh. I've missed her, and she has to know how I feel about her by now. The void in my soul has filled now that we're back. The tightness in my chest and sucky days without her have lifted and I can't wait for us to catch up on lost time. I need her in my life, she's always there for me and I've gotten used to seeing her every day. We just click as friends, and who knows if one day we'll be more than that to each other.

"What do you think you're doing?" Her smile does something to me. She deserves to smile every day.

"Just getting comfortable." I lean back in my seat and adjust my lap belt, never moving my hand from her leg in the process. She slides her hand over mine and pulls out onto the highway.

My house is only about five miles from here, and I'm glad this'll be a short trip. I'd like to feel her against me again.

"So, did you miss me?" I begin to tease her, hoping she admits to it.

"Oh yeah. You know I did."

"What did you miss most?"

"Your killer guitar skills for sure."

"Ah. That's all I'm worth to ya! I see how you are." She turns to look at me. The lights shine on her face and I can see an expression that says so much more. The look in her eye speaks volumes, and I'm not going to lie, it feels good to see her look at me like that.

We hold the look a little longer before I notice the lights getting brighter on her face. I glance forward and see headlights aiming right in our direction. Yelling at her to watch out pulls her attention back to the road.

Everything begins to move in slow motion. I watch her grab the wheel with both hands and try to divert the car, but it's too late. The impact is vicious. I'll never forget the feeling of the air bag exploding and the seatbelt restricting my movement forward.

We begin to spin, and the next thing I remember is the music blaring and everything else going completely quiet. I open my eyes after…I'm not sure how long…and slide my hand over to feel for her. I turn my head in search of her and realize the severity of the situation very quickly. Her leg is covered in blood and her face looks terrified. I move to unbuckle my seatbelt and fight the airbag in the process. I can tell my body is injured, but my adrenaline has taken over.

I reach for her only to find my worst nightmare is coming true. She runs her hand over her stomach, filling it with blood before she starts to cry. Her eyes are pleading with me to save her and there's nothing I can do. There's blood everywhere.

Listening to the sirens coming near, I pull up in my seat to hold her. There isn't much room to maneuver, but I do the best I can. I guide her face to look at me. She finds my eyes and we both cry.

"Lilly. I'm sorry I never told you how much I love you. You have to hang on. The ambulance is on its way and they'll help you." Her eyes fill with tears and she leans forward placing her lips on mine. The only thing I can do is kiss her soft lips and pray to God that she's not taken from me.

We stay like this for what seems like a few minutes, yet only seconds at the same time. I pull away to look at her when her face begins to rest on mine. She takes one last breath and my life crashes before my eyes. I continue to hold her as my screams echo over the sounds surrounding us.

My tears blind me as I try to take in her face while I have a chance. I notice the metal in her stomach and begin to scream even louder in hysterics. *What the fuck is happening?*

The medics rush to the scene and begin to talk to me. I don't even know what they're saying to me, but I just tell them to save her.

"Save her. That's all I need. Save her. Don't worry about me. Save her. Please God, save her."

"Sir, we need you to cooperate so we can get to her." Placing one more kiss to her forehead, I let them remove me from the car.

Everything is numb. I feel nothing.

I hear nothing.

I smell nothing,

I see nothing.

They begin strapping me to the gurney in every possible way. There's even a neck brace, which I'm sure I don't need, but I don't care. They can't possibly fix what hurts most. There is no brace or surgery that can repair what's happened tonight.

The ambulance ride to the hospital is rushed and the medics seem to be moving around me quite a bit. Their voices make noise, but not sense. I begin to nod off in hopes of waking up from this nightmare.

Waking up in this much pain should be illegal. I move my head, trying to see who the sobbing is coming from. Eaven has her legs tucked up in a chair, crying her eyes out. She's as devastated as I feel, and it worries me. My fear is that what I remember is what truly happened. I don't want to hear that Lilly is gone forever. How am I supposed to care about anything if that's the case?

"Hey, you. You're awake." Ev's words are soft and her voice is restricted.

"Yeah." That's all I've got. There isn't any other conversation left in me. I listen to the sound of the nurse moving around me, taking my vitals and talking chart bullshit. Talon comes into the room and whispers to Eaven, and they both wrap each other up for a hug and proceed to cry even more. I know what this means.

She's gone.

I listen to Eaven break down and a little more of me dies with each cry that slips out of her mouth. The pain in her sobs can only be matched with the pain I'm feeling inside.

I try to lift up in the bed and my body tells me to fuck off. I'm sore as hell and can hardly move. She notices me trying to move and starts to get a nurse.

"No." Ev stops in her tracks.

"Just set me up higher." She starts to adjust the bed without ever looking at me. I want her to look at me and tell me Lilly is okay. Tell me that this is all a horrible nightmare and I was in a car accident all by myself.

"Tell me." She clenches her eyes closed and begins to let the tears roll again. I look in the room for Talon, but he's not here anymore.

"Ev. Tell me Lilly is okay." She doesn't. Her attempt to comfort me by grabbing my hand isn't working. Her grip on my hand is tight and her actions are doing the talking for her.

I can't breathe past the brick in my throat. How could this happen? Everything was starting to work in our favor and now she's gone. How will I ever learn to live without her when the last few days without her have been hell?

"Who was driving the other car?"

She struggles past some cries before she manages to say, "A drunk driver crossed the median."

Memories of me distracting her come to surface, and the image of her smiling face flashes before my eyes. How could something so beautiful be taken away so harshly?

She was so young and had never been treated like she deserved. How can I ever forgive myself for not telling her how I felt about her?

Talon walks in and pulls Ev in for a hug. He looks over at me and I can see nothing but sympathy. His stare doesn't accuse me, but I can't keep eye contact with him. I know this is my fault.

"Talon. Tell me."

"She's gone, man." Assuming and officially hearing are completely different. His words confirm it. I can hardly handle this information. To say I'm losing my shit is an understatement.

My breathing becomes rapid and everything begins to hurt even worse. I can't fucking see through the tears draining from my eyes and I can't feel anything past the pain in my chest.

Nausea takes over and I begin vomiting shortly after. A nurse starts to adjust some of the machines attached to me and it isn't long before I'm falling asleep again. Sleep is much better than the reality of this.

Every time I wake up I ask for pain medicine. It's easier to deal with when I'm out cold. I have no idea how many days and nights go by like this. My mom and either Ev or Ivy are here every time I wake up. It's usually Ev, and she doesn't even try to talk to me about Lilly. She tries to talk about the weather and things that aren't worth a damn.

I don't have the energy for small talk or being polite about anything. The day the nurse forces me out of bed, I decide to ask Ev questions.

"When's the funeral?"

"Tomorrow."

"Did that asshole make it?"

"No. He died on impact." I should be banned to hell for my thoughts and I'm not sure I won't be in the end.

"I need to get out of here before the funeral."

"I asked the doctor if you'd be able to attend and he thinks you'll be released tomorrow. If not, he'll try to work something out so you can get to the funeral."

"I can't believe this is happening."

"I know, Luke."

This last night in the hospital is the worst. I begin to feel the pain all over my body. I'm bruised across my chest and there are multiple cuts all over me. The doctors are worried about internal bleeding and it doesn't help that I'm not psychologically ready to be released.

Holden, Talon, Taron, and Ivy all come with Eaven to pick me up from the hospital. My parents understand my need to be with the group today.

"We're going to need each other to get through this day," Talon speaks first. The thought of getting through the day isn't even logical. How do we say goodbye to someone who means so much to us?

"I got you a suit for today. You're a pall bearer." Eaven wraps me up in a hug.

"I need to go by her house. There's something I need to get." No one objects, probably because they can hardly hear me over this fucking permanent lump in my throat.

I'm finally released with only two hours before the service. We race to her house, and it nearly tears us all apart when we pull in to the driveway. I use my key and open the door, instantly smelling a hint of her perfume in the air.

Biting down and refusing a complete breakdown quite yet, I go straight for her room. She has two guitars and I need them both. I throw both over my shoulder and take one last look around her bedroom. Memories of her surround me and I fight like hell to keep it together long enough to make it through this day.

Closing my eyes to block the tears, I turn to walk out of her house. I lock the door and quickly jump back in Talon's truck. The others don't say a word to me. That's the problem—none of us know what to say. There's nothing that can be said to make her come back to us. We stop at my house so I can change and clean up.

The funeral home is packed when we arrive. I grab one guitar and leave the other one behind. We all walk in together, but they all stay behind when I begin to walk toward her. Her casket is open and I can see her face over the edge as soon as I walk in the door.

She's so pale and looks nothing like herself. I fight to find the strength to hold it together, but this shit is getting to me. How do I say goodbye to my best friend? The only woman I've learned to love. Regret washes over me at a lethal rate as I stand there and take in everything my eyes will allow me to see past the tears.

I open the case to her stage guitar and pull off the strap, placing it in my pocket. I start strumming her song slowly, trying like hell to get through it perfectly. The people in the foyer begin to listen, but I don't care to play for anyone but her today.

I play through the song three times before I kiss the strings and slide the guitar into her casket. I move her cold hands over the neck of the guitar and position them so that she's holding it. It's only fitting that she be holding her passion when she goes.

The funeral falls upon deaf ears of mine. The words that are spoken don't sink in at all as I sit there, a shell of myself through the whole thing. We move her body to the hearse and then again over the hole at the grave site. I sprinkle dirt over her when it's time and then turn to walk away from everything. I grab her guitar out of Talon's truck and never turn back.

I keep walking until I make it to my house, staying just long enough to pack a large bag and lock up everything.

Epilogue

Luke

Life can change in a heartbeat. Everything you know can become a memory, and the future can be left in the hands of something greater than you can control.

My life changed the second her heart stopped beating. I haven't felt anything since she took her last breath. Leaving the band and everything I knew before was imperative. I can hardly live with myself, so how do I expect the others to live around me?

My cell phone is in the bottom of a river somewhere between Missouri and California. The last thing I want to do is talk about it with anyone. The endless list of girls isn't welcome, either. The thought of my old lifestyle repulses me and I have no idea how to overcome all of this.

I work and sleep. Every day.

It's been six months since I sprinkled dirt over her casket and said goodbye to my best friend in life. I have so many regrets when it comes to her. I've played the 'if I would've' game over and over, coming up with the same conclusion every time. I fucked up. She died not knowing how I truly felt about her. Would we have ended up in love, together forever? We will never know.

I know that I loved that girl and I had no idea what I had until it was gone. Her heart was truly amazing and she was a huge inspiration to me. I've never had anyone care for me so deeply and only want what was in my best interest. I'll never forget her or our friendship we shared.

I kept her old guitar, and every once in a while I get it out to strum a few songs, hoping she can feel what I'm trying to say.

I've learned a lesson in all of this....

Life is short, but regret seems to last forever.

Note from the author: Luke's story isn't over, check out the preview to book 4 in the series. Coming Spring 2014!

*****Please** don't spoil the book for everyone by giving away the twist in your review.

Thanks ~ Hilary

Coming Soon

Fighting the Odds

Luke

The mundane repetition of my life is exactly what I deserve. I'm taking each day at a time and it doesn't help that I can't shake the guilt of not telling Lilly how I felt when I had the time.

Tonight is the first night I've been anywhere besides the gym or in my tiny apartment. I work twelve-hour shifts at the factory and barely bring home enough money to pay my bills. The royalties from the music collect in my bank account, but I refuse to touch them. I don't want *anything* that'll remind me of my past.

Music is a huge problem for me. Every song either reminds me of her, or it's something that 'Rebel Walking' played at one time. The worst was when I heard *her* song on the radio. I didn't realize they were going to actually release it after everything that happened.

Parking is ridiculous at the coliseum, so I choose to jog the five miles instead. This fight is supposed to be between two of the best in the division. There was an advertisement for it in the gym and I thought it would be interesting to see how it plays out. Both of these guys are stacked, so it's not like there's a clear cut favorite. Sure, fans are screaming for each of them, but I'm not impressed enough with either to care who wins.

I watch the fight inside the crowd of crazy fans. The irony of being on this side of the show isn't lost on me. Neither one of the fighters takes the fight and it comes down to a split decision between the judges. The fans go wild when Greg ‘The Punisher' Mills takes the victory.

The people don't start to file out for a long time, and I'm in no hurry to leave, either. People-watching has become a past time of mine, and there's no reason for me to rush home to the empty walls that confine me every night.

Waiting ‘til most of the crowd files out, I decide to go around the back of the building to miss all the traffic. As soon as I turn the corner I can hear an idiot yelling obscenities, so I look toward the open door to see a man slap a smaller figure across the face.

I try to calm my inner rage until I get close enough to see what's going on. All I can see is someone shorter than him, with a hood on, cowering down from his blows.

"Kimber, you're just a fucking slut. How many did you fuck? You let them look at you and I'm fucking tired of it." He backhands her this time and gets in a punch to her stomach before I can reach him.

Yanking him into the dark alley, I tear into this man. I can't fucking handle when a guy hits a girl for *any* reason. I punch him over and over in the face until he falls to the ground and then pull him into a headlock.

"Why don't you hit someone your own fucking size, asshole? I'm waiting." Blood covers my fists and I keep going until he finally stops fighting me. I know he's passed out, but anger is still flowing through me. Hell, I haven't felt anything in months, and right now I'm a whole fucking array of emotions.

I climb up off the ground and move to check on her. Her cries gut me and I don't even know her. I slide her hood down off her head and see the bruising already. Her face is swollen and her lip is bleeding and this pisses me off even more.

"Can I take you somewhere?"

"No, he'll just find me." Her voice is so small and weak that I struggle to hear her. The door slams open and I instinctively shield her. A guy in a suit walks over to the idiot on the ground and checks his pulse. When he finds one, he moves to face me and the girl disappears through the doorway.

"What's your name?"

"I don't have one."

"You just took out my top fighter, what's your fucking name?"

"I don't fucking have one."

This novel featured a crossover from Lexi Buchanan's Spicy.

To read more about Callie and the members of Destruction check out Lexi's books!

Bad Boy Rocker's Series Order

Sizzle

Spicy

Acknowledgments

First and always, I'd like to thank my husband for allowing me to live my dream and supporting me completely. I could never publish if it weren't for this man. He takes on so much just so that I can get each novel out. He is the man of my dreams and I couldn't imagine doing anything without him. Because of him, my kids love that their mom has a passion for her work. It means everything to me that I can show them to live their dreams, even when those dreams change over time.

Jake Wilson.... How in the hell did the two of us match up? I couldn't ask for a better muse to travel with. You're a badass and the smartest decision I ever made was locking you in the second I saw you! I'm proud and excited to see where we've come since the train depot, and I know we're only beginning. It'll be an adventure and I'm happy to share it with a great friend.

Tynna.... As always, you saved my tail during the writing of this novel. Without you, I could never keep up with everything. You keep me organized, even though it's a challenge. Thank you for all that you do behind the scenes!

Julie.... Love our talks and you get me, crazy bitch and all. You are probably the only person I can call with the insanity I did, and not get judged! Instead, you encourage the craze, and for this I love you! One day I'll make that story happen and we'll sit back and watch the buzz around it and laugh with our fireball in hand. Thank you for helping me with my storylines!

Christine... Your support is unending and I'm happy we met how we did! Not many can say something that hilarious sparked up a friendship like we have. I value your opinion and you're always there to hear me out! One of these days, I'm going to visit you up north and I promise, we'll have the best time ever!

Golden & Laura... You guys complete my covers and I couldn't be more excited when I get stuff from you both! You do an outstanding job and it's pure perfection when we finish! Thanks for being awesome and great at what you do!

Tiffany... My editor... thanks for taking my raw work and polishing it up! I put you on the craziest time constraints and you always pull through for me. Not many other editors would do that and that's why you and I work well together!

My street team... These girls are always there promoting me, even when the buzz has fallen. I couldn't ask for a better group and that's why I never add to it. Why mess with perfection?

Don't Close Your Eyes

By Hilary Storm

Short Story available in the Anthology 'Pink Shades of Words' until May 31st, 2014

(All proceeds go to breast cancer research)

Full novel coming Summer 2014

Chapter One

These bags are extremely heavy. I should've asked Scott to help me, but I'd hate to inconvenience him and his new wife. There really isn't anyone else to call for help since they've all stepped out of my 'crazy' world; the sudden changes I made scared everyone off. I can still hear their comments about how unstable I am. 'Who quits their job to write a book?' Yeah, well bitches, I did. I've written five novels in a series and I have plans for so many more, but none of them know that. They seriously think I sit here in my apartment and grieve.

I didn't become a New York Times bestselling author by crying myself to sleep at night. I don't have time for tears; there are places to go and people to meet. I'm headed to a book signing in New York City. It's a privilege to even be invited to this event. A part of me is excited and another is dreading this day.

I just wish I could have one more day with him. I'd love to show him that I'm doing it, even though our friends and family have zero faith in me. He always believed in me and supported me in everything I set out to do. Very few people find a person who truly comes through for them when they have off the wall ideas. You know, like work as an accountant for six years and then one day decide you'd like to write a book. I guess it didn't help that I decided to do that exactly one month from the day he died.

He would've been one hundred percent behind me, but he's not here, so I go it alone. Don't get me wrong, I miss him like crazy, but that won't bring him back to me. As for everyone else, they stepped away from me when I needed the support the most. They got off this crazy train and it doesn't circle back around to pick up passengers who jump ship. Scott's the only one who has had much to do with me since I 'went crazy'.

To be honest, my emotions were so out of control that it took me spilling it all onto paper for me to be able to cope with everything. I miss him so much and everyone wants me to 'talk' about it. I just can't and it's easier to work through my demons on my own.

I finally work my way past airport security after checking my luggage. Obviously, security isn't getting any easier to pass through because I had to be scanned separately from the others. It's probably because they sense the 'crazy' that the others speak of. This loneliness is partly my fault, but it would've been nice for them to believe in me a *little*.

The flight is full of people and should be interesting. I haven't been in a crowd of people since the funeral almost a year ago. This is a big step for me, though. A book signing in New York City is huge for an author to attend, never mind the fact that I've always wanted to go there. James and I talked about traveling there together many times.

I sit in my window seat and hope for the peace I need to stay focused on my inner strength to get through this weekend. My ear buds begin to blare one of my favorite Hinder songs and I pull my magazine out of my bag to stay entertained for the non-stop flight across the states.

The passengers keep piling in and I begin to wonder just how large this airplane is. I paid extra money to fly First Class in hopes of staying under the radar of any chatty passengers and kids that don't mind their parents.

I'm trying to stay focused on my article while someone is reaching over my head to load his luggage, completely distracting me. I really should've purchased the seat next to me. *Why didn't I think of that before now?* Even with the help of the flight attendant he has to force the bags into the compartment. *How the hell much stuff does he have?*

I purposely don't make eye contact with him after he flops into the seat right beside mine. His leg pushes against mine a few times and he seems extremely restless. I'm not sure it's intentional, but it seems that way.

We begin to prepare for take off so I pull out my ear buds to hear all of the safety information. Watching and listening to the flight attendant give her instructions kind of overwhelms me, but

I'm sure it'll all come to me in case of a true emergency. It's not like we'll survive if this huge bird has a real emergency anyway.

I slip the buds back in for take off and begin to read again. It isn't until he presses his leg into mine again that I begin to get irritated. His posture is slouched and he's noticeably oblivious to the fact that he's invading my space with his legs spread open like that.

"Excuse me." I yank out an ear bud and let it fall against my chest while I use my hand to gesture toward his leg. I'm sure my face is telling him exactly how I feel, because it never lies. I have a very shitty poker face.

"No worries. You're not bothering me." The shock on my face from his audacity has him smiling.

"You're bothering me. So if you don't mind, please move your leg." I sit back in hopes of him doing as I ask and grab the ear bud to reposition.

"Nah. I don't mind. Sorry, ma'am." *Ah HELL NO. He did NOT just call me ma'am.* That makes me feel so damn old. I choose to attempt to ignore him and move to plug my ear again, but *hell* if it doesn't bother me. His stare begins to heat my skin—you know, like the weird feeling you get when you can tell someone is watching you. I shift so that I'm turned more toward the window and try to enjoy the view of the landscape below. The feel of his leg brushing up against mine again causes me to pull further away from him. I notice the touch of his finger on my shoulder and everything inside of me wants to stand up and scream for this creep to get off of me. My head whips around to glare at him when I notice the attendant staring at me in the aisle.

"Would you care for something to drink?"

"Yes, I'll take a water, please."

"One water, one Jack and Coke. I'll be right back." Why do I let it shock me that this character is drinking at 8:30 in the morning? It really shouldn't shock me at all.

"Don't you think it's kind of early to be drinking like that?"

"It's okay. I drink Coke any time of day!"

"Right.... Well, good luck with that."

"You're pretty stiff. You could probably use a drink like that yourself!"

"I'm not stiff, so keep your comments to yourself, if you don't mind."

"I think you *are* stiff and you have to live a little, but I'll work on keeping that to myself." *Who does he think he is?* He doesn't get to judge me after only sitting beside me for a couple of minutes.

"You have no idea what I'm going through, so don't try to judge me based on the few minutes you've seen me today."

"Touché. Let me apologize and maybe we can start over." I wait for his actual apology and find myself waiting too long. My impatience grows wild and I can't believe I'm letting this guy really get to me. He enjoys my silence a little longer before he finally speaks.

"I'm truly sorry for calling you stiff. Please accept my apology and let me buy you a drink." He watches my face very closely and must finally get a clue that he's pissing on a ticking time bomb. He extends his hand in an introduction-like stance.

"Liam Brooks." The disgust on my face *has* to be obvious as I refuse to shake his hand or willingly touch anything of his. His sexy as hell grin flashes across his face and damn if my eyes don't betray me. Those lips are the kind you want to watch someone run their tongue over. There is an awkward silence before I begin to reach out to accept his introduction.

"Olivia Drake." My eyes get caught up in his gorgeous baby blues for a few seconds before I realize our hands are still touching. I pull back slowly and shift back in my seat.

"Olivia Drake, what has you headed to New York City?" Telling a stranger any more about myself is *completely* out of the question, so I quickly decide to be as vague as possible.

"Business trip."

"Me, too. Do you travel there often?"

"No, this is my first time."

The drinks arrive and he immediately asks for a second drink of the same. "The lady will have what I'm having." His persistence is such a pain in my ass. This flight is going to be torture if I continue to let him get to me so I send the flight attendant a smile in agreement.

He leans back in his seat in such a relaxed state next to my very straight, upright and uptight posture. Taking note of that makes me realize I *am* stiff and tense. I prefer to call it focused and driven, but those words don't really explain my posture.

I try to relax a bit by leaning the seat back and decide to prove to myself that I'm not *stiff.* He offers me the Jack and Coke just as I have this epiphany so I gladly accept his challenge.

Chapter Two

The smell reminds me of him. James loved Jack and Coke. I close my eyes and inhale the memorable scent before I swallow my first sip. The liquor is so strong that it causes me to cough. His laughter pulls my attention from the memories.

"Glad you find this funny."

"Your expressions are very dramatic and I can tell exactly what you're thinking."

"Really? What am I thinking right now?"

"You're thinking.... 'This jackass thinks he's fucking suave and he's nothing but a piece of shit on the bottom of my shoe.'.... aren't you?"

"Well hell. You *can* read my mind!" His drink arrives and he turns to face me.

"To not forgetting to live life." I try to figure out how, less than an hour ago, I was fighting with my luggage by myself and now I'm drinking to *living life* with a stranger.

"To living life." This sip goes down a little better, probably because I get a little lost looking at him again. His dark, messy hair *does not* have me wanting to run my fingers through it. The sleeves of his tight t-shirt aren't so tight that I can see his muscles bulging and I sure as hell *don't* want to see what else is under that shirt. Not. At. All.

My eyes travel back up to his face just in time to see that he's enjoying the view as well. Sitting back quickly, I pull my shirt up a little to hide any cleavage that's showing. *What am I doing? Why am I reacting like this with a complete stranger?* Guilt reigns over me for the next few minutes. I try to process the reasons that I feel like this. It's been a long time for me and I know that's part of it. James and I had a very active sex life and I've really isolated myself since his death. I must be sex starved; that would explain why my thoughts are complete chaos right now.

What frustrates me a little is the fact that I know this guy knows he's affecting me like this. Really, what's the harm in flirting with this guy? It's not like I'll ever see him again. This drought could go on for a decade if I don't let myself feel every once in awhile. *What if?*

What if I let this guy into my life just long enough for some fun and he rocks my world just like I crave? What if he rocks it so hard that I forget my damn name and where I live, which is all totally possible. Writing romance novels really *does* get to a girl after a while.

What if I try to get somewhere with him and he rejects me? Can my ego take that right now? Being an author really messes with your self confidence and actually traveling to New York at this moment has me nervous if I think about it at all.

What if we have sex and he decides he wants to see me again? That can't happen. Listen to me! I'm already plotting how the story will go and I've hardly said a word to him.

What if I put my ear bud back in and ignore his pompous ass for the rest of the flight and write him into my next novel? I could kill him off in the first chapter just to prove a point. I'll make it gruesome and let it be at the hands of the strong female character.

"What kind of business in New York?" He attempts to strike up the conversation once again. I could tell him that I'm an author, but why tell a complete stranger how to actually find you if he chooses to search for you?

"I'm an accountant. There's a conference I have to attend." Neither of those statements are a lie, yet I think they *will* manage to keep my information private.

"Nice. I'm terrible with numbers."

"Yeah, luckily it comes easily to me. What about you?"

"Business as well. I'm doing research for a project that I'm working on."

"Oooooh. Intriguing. You have my attention now! What kind of project would have you traveling to the big city?"

"Family stuff. I promised a loved one that I'd follow up on something very important, and here I am doing what I promised."

"Man of your word, then."

"Most definitely." Okay, this is good for me. Honesty is very important to me, not that I'm looking for a relationship with him, though.

"So tell me, Miss Drake, did it hurt?" *Hurt? What is he talking about*?

"Not sure what you're asking."

"When you fell from heaven." Oh great! A corny ass pick up line. My laughter becomes obnoxious before I have a chance to stop myself.

"Don't be so sure that's where I'm from!"

"I can tell you're one of those good girls, straight out of the book. You don't get out much and you're okay with that. You probably stay home on the weekends and work." I really hate that I'm this transparent.

"Well, *I* can tell that you get around and probably use lame ass pick up lines on girls after getting them drunk, just so you can get laid."

"Damn. You see right through my plan!" My face lights up with a smile. Actually, it's one of the first smiles I've had in a very long time. "You have a very nice smile. You really should smile more often." His words make me stop and think about my life for a second. I really *don't* take the time to smile. My life revolves around being an author and living vicariously through my characters. My reason for smiling is gone and I can't really do anything to get that back.

"Yeah, well I'll try to work on that."

"I always try to find at least one thing every day that'll make me smile." I choose not to tell him how lonely my life is and that there really isn't a reason to smile outside of my success as an author. Our conversation stops for a few minutes while the attendants serve the complimentary snacks. I shove mine in my bag, knowing New York City is a big place and I'll probably opt out of leaving the hotel in search of food.

"So, Livi, tell me more about yourself." I pause in thought as my mind runs wild with reasons to shut him off from any actual information about myself, but my gut feelings about him win over. Livi as a nickname kind of grew on me when it came across his lips.

"I'm a single, hard working woman who stays at home on weekends and works. I live in Phoenix and I have a dream of traveling the world one day."

"Very nice! I knew I was right about you. Where would you like to travel?"

"Oh, you know, London, Paris, Australia, Canada. Really my list could go on forever. I just want to see places that I've heard so much about."

"Sounds like you need a bucket list."

"Yeah, I guess you could say I already have one. One day I'll be able to do some of the things I have planned."

"I hope so."

"How about you? I've shared a few of my secrets, now it's your turn."

"I'm a single, hard working guy who doesn't stay at home on weekends and I also live in Phoenix, but I'm originally from

Denver. I've traveled quite a bit in my life, but not for enjoyment. Maybe one day I'll be able to travel for leisure. I have four brothers and we all work together."

"That's awesome! I wish I had a brother."

"There have been days where I would've let you have them. But all in all, I'd do anything for every single one of them." He's so serious now that he's talking about his family. His mind seems to wander for a brief second before he quickly returns to give me his full attention again.

"I'd give anything for a family." My statement is cut off by the announcement that our plane will soon be entering turbulence. The thought of a rough flight doesn't settle well with me. I start to look through my phone for another song to play. I'm so used to having music on all day.

"What are ya listening to?"

"I have a huge play list, I'm just scrolling through."

"Let me choose a song for you." His finger brushes over mine when he reaches for the phone. I glance down as he removes the phone from my hand and notice his leg bumped up against mine again, but this time it doesn't irritate me.

He scrolls through my music and I watch as he hesitates, but I can't see what he's looking at. "Okay. You ready?" The song begins and an instant rush of heat flows through my body. There is no mistaking that beat. I'm not sure where the grin on my face comes from, but it spreads across my lips. I begin to move my leg with the beat, closing my eyes and allowing the music move me. It's impossible not to move your body to this song. He really did just play 'Closer' by Nine Inch Nails to me. I'm going to take this as a sign that we will be pushing this a little further than conversation.

I listen to the entire song while he watches my every move. I can feel him adjust in his seat a few times while the music moves me. The pressure of his body leaning on mine gives me hope for what's to come.

When the song finishes, I don't really know how to react, so I begin to scroll again. The sexual tension is so damn tight right now I can hardly breathe and I know *he* feels it, too.

"What hotel are you staying at?" His whisper in my ear sends a chill straight through to my core.

"Downtown Marriott." My breathy answer proves to him that I'm game for anything. He hasn't pulled away from my face since whispering in my ear. I let my eyes move up his chest, over his lips and to his eyes. His close proximity has me holding my breath for sure. His eyes begin to move over my features right before he sits back in his seat. He's still leaning in my direction, but not right in my face so I can finally take a much needed breath of air.

The rest of the flight seems to go extremely fast and it isn't long before we land. I spend the remainder of the time contemplating what I'm about to do. It's been almost a year since James passed, but I still really miss him. I think knowing that this will be nothing more than a one-time hookup will work for me. Anything more than that and I know I'll have a hard time,

There really isn't any further conversation between us until I step into the airport. "I'll help you with your luggage and then we can get a cab to your hotel room." He stands right behind me while we are waiting for the luggage to arrive. I'm talking *right* behind me and I'm guessing it's to hide the bulge that I can feel against my ass. Shit, it's been a long time and I want to do this. I refuse to let myself begin to think about my past and reasons why this shouldn't happen.

Shattered and Shaken
Shaken Series
Book 1
Written by J Bailes

Chapter 1- Shaken

WAKING UP TO SORE muscles and a tight chest, my body feels like it's been torn to pieces. My head hurts, my heart aches, and my soul is shattered. The sun is unwanted, shining bright into my eyes. The loud joyful chirping of birds infuriates me.

Fighting against the sun, I force my eyes open and look at my surroundings, praying I'm lost in a nightmare. The events from this week remain fresh in my mind, and I'm having difficulty grasping the concept that Kyle's never coming home. The thought of never seeing him again is unbearable. Not only was he my brother, he was my best friend, my provider: my everything.

How could he leave me? He had promised to come home safely; he promised to think of me and push through whatever came his way. He lied. I'm hurt, but I'm also livid that he could be so selfish. When Kyle decided to join the military, he didn't consider the emotional hell he'd inflict on Mom and I; he didn't give a flying fuck about either one of our opinions. Kyle was as stubborn as a mule, and once he had his mind set on something, he made it happen - no matter what the consequences were. Prime example, him joining the military. I pleaded for him to stay, but he didn't, and look what his stubbornness resulted in - death. Now he's gone and we have no one!

Our father was diagnosed with stage-four lung cancer my junior year of high school, and Kyle's sophomore year of college. Dad's physician estimated he would live no more than six months, but he was a fighter and determined to prove them wrong. The cancer was so advanced the physicians were uncomfortable providing him with chemotherapy treatments. The doctors had explained that chemo wouldn't cure his cancer, but there was a possibility it could help prolong his life. Despite the physicians' beliefs, dad decided to give chemo a try, but it made him deathly ill.

After six months of treatment and a two-week hospital stay, he decided to let the cancer run its natural course. Dad thrived to live, but unfortunately, he died eighteen months later. Mom, Kyle, and I watched as dad withered away to nothing. The tall, dark, and handsome man I knew as the strongest man in the world had turned brittle and weak. His thick curly locks disappeared, his broad body frame became narrow, and his muscles deteriorated. As days passed and the cancer spread, dad's will to live diminished. We stood by him and held his hand as he struggled to take his last breath; it was the most painful experience I've ever encountered - until now.

After our father's death, mom took on a second job to pay for his medical bills. It seems that insurance companies only want to provide their services to healthy patients. Get sick and they kick your ass off the policy faster than you can blink. We were determined to beat cancer's ass.

Mom had to refinance the house and take out several high interest loans so that dad could receive his treatments, home health, and follow-up doctor visits, putting her eyeball deep in debt. She worked as a nurse for the local emergency room every Monday, Wednesday, and Friday nights. The other nights, she worked as a private nurse caring for patients with disabilities. Before our father became ill, Mom was gorgeous, sporting healthy long brown waves, glowing sun-kissed skin, vibrant green eyes, and a nice toned body. But depression set in, and with the stress of two jobs, mom's great looks and enthusiasm diminished. Her hair became brittle; her appetite vanished, and she lost an absurd amount of weight. Her cheeks sunk in, while her skin paled, and her eyes lost their shine. In all honesty, she looked like shit. Don't get me wrong, I mourned the loss of my father, but life moves on. Kyle mourned and moved on, but seeing Mom worn out and defeated made Kyle take matters into his own hands. He knew the true reason mom had to work two jobs.

Mom was a Dave Ramsey graduate, and she refused to let us take out student loans. She was being unrealistic believing I could pay cash for college. Dad's insurance policy expired before he died, and the money left from his 401k was only enough to pay for one of our tuitions. Since Kyle was oldest, it belonged to him. Kyle wouldn't allow me to skip college. He put his foot down and demanded Mom drop her second job. He advised her to take his tuition money and invest it into my education. He had made the decision after he had met with military recruiters. They fed his brain with lies, luring him into their trap; it was all bullshit. If being 'Army strong" is such a great thing, then why must you sign a contract with your blood, huh? What other job requires you to sign a minimum four-year contract to offer up your life? Go ahead, I'll wait...not a damn one. Their contract isn't one you can breach and be forced to pay fines or anything like that. You go AWOL and breach your contract, your ass is going to jail. The only pro of enlisting into the military is that it's a career that requires no experience, and they pay a decent salary for you becoming a life-offering slave, simply my opinion.

I remained bitter for a while, but eventually, I'd adjusted to Kyle's absence; his first deployment was the most difficult. Normally, he was deployed for seven months at a time, give or take a few months. We talked to each other over the phone almost every morning. We got to speak to one another for about ten minutes, sometime less; they were the minutes I craved each day. Hearing his voice put my nerves at ease; I loved that man more than most siblings will ever admit. Every once in a while, we'd Skype, but those conversations were even shorter. Soldiers would be lined up waiting to see their families, so we made our conversations quick.

I loved seeing Kyle over the screen, but I'd hate to be the reason a child didn't get to see their mom or dad for what could possibly be their last time. The worst part of Kyle being overseas was playing the waiting game. When someone was killed in the line of duty, their systems would shut down for two weeks, or until the next of kin were notified. The silence was debilitating, and I absolutely hated waiting to hear his voice. When the phone rang and I finally heard his voice, I would fall to my knees and cry. I'd cried for the loss of soldiers. I cried for their families, but mostly, I cried out of happiness, because Kyle's heart continued beating.

I stop myself from reminiscing and untangle from my sheets. I sit up and my muscles scream out in protest. Sitting still, I allow them to adjust to the position before slinging my legs off the bed and attempting to stand. Reaching my arms above my head, I stretch out soreness that has consumed my muscles. Strolling towards my bedroom window, I pull the curtain aside and reach down to slide the window open. It's beautiful out. The sun is brightly shining. The air is warm with a slight breeze, and I hear laughter of playing children. Really?
What is Mother Nature thinking? It shouldn't be gorgeous the day after I buried one of the most important people in my life. Kyle's death is devastating and the world moves on as if nothing's happened. I feel as if Mother Nature should be unleashing her wrath on Earth. There should be heavy downpours of rain that cause floods, rolls of Earth-shaking thunder, damaging winds and lightning strikes catching shit on fire: anything but sunny. A piece of me wants someone to feel the tiniest ounce of pain my mother and I are experiencing, but another piece of me wouldn't wish this pain on my worst enemy. Tears prick my eyes, and I attempt to take in a few deep breaths but fail. As soon as I suck in the air, I bust into heart-wrenching sobs. Why is this happening to me? Did I not experience enough heartache watching my father lose his battle to cancer?

As I press my back against the wall and slide down to the floor, my hands cover my face and I scream out every bit of pain that's within me. I don't stop until my tears run dry and I'm gasping for air. I try to focus on breathing but it's difficult. My sadness has turned into complete anger and I have the urge to break things, anything. I push myself up off the floor and punch at the air. I look around my room for something to smash, but there's nothing. Looking over to my side, I see picture frames filled with Kyle's smiling face; seeing him causes my heart to clench and pain surges through my veins. Jumping onto my bed, I reach over and forcefully swipe my arm across the nightstand, successfully knocking every picture of me and Kyle to the hardwood floor.

The frames break apart and the glass shatters. Immediately, I regret breaking them, but there's something about the sound of shattering glass that makes my chest feel lighter, making it easier to breathe. I should feel some sort of remorse by not wanting to look at Kyle's face, but at the moment, my heart can't tolerate the slightest glimpse of him. I'd rather surrender myself to the pain of a thousand hornet stings than to feel the pain I get when looking at someone I know I'll never see again.

I gather some towels and head towards the bathroom. Laying my towels on top of the vanity, I glance into the mirror. I look like shit. My hair's in knots and matted to the side of my face. My eyes are red and swollen, and my cheeks are tear stained with smeared mascara. I turn towards the shower and turn the water to its hottest setting, praying the heat will ease my aches and pains. I wait a few moments before sticking my hand under the water to test the temperature; it's hot but tolerable.

Gently pulling the shower curtain aside, I submerge myself into the heat. It's friggin' hot! It stings like a mother, but eventually, my body adjusts to the temperature, and the stinging becomes bearable. I reach around and hold my hair up so the pressure from the water can beat against my neck. I roll my neck in circular motions trying to release the tension, but as I let the water relax me, I have flashbacks from the day Kyle was supposed to return home.

"I can't wait to see the look on his face when he gets home," mom exclaims. "I can't believe he's been gone for seven months, feels longer." The smile she's wearing is bigger than the state of Texas, and it's contagious.

"It's probably because we haven't spoken to him in over a week," I suggest, blowing a piece of hair out of my face as I hang balloons.

"Yeah, wonder what's taking them so long to notify the family? I hate this, ya know...anxiously waiting to see if we'll get a call with

his sweet voice on the other end, or if we'll be getting an unwanted knock at our door," she says, her smile disappearing as her eyes begin to mist.

I stop hanging balloons and step down from the stool to walk over and embrace her in a tight hug "Look here, Lucy, don't you go gettin' all sappy on me now," I pucker, using my best Ricky Ricardo impersonation - Dad did it constantly. "Kyle's fine. He's probably gettin' off the plane now and heading over to base. He'll be home soon," I urge, squeezing her tightly.

She takes in a deep breath and nods her head "You're right. He'll be here shortly, so we better get busy." She loosens our hug, backs away and makes her way into the kitchen. "Oh, and Allie, you call me by any name other than Mom again...I'll cut off all your funds," she informs over her shoulder, her smile reappearing.

It's close to five thirty and people from our neighborhood begin to show up. The doorbell won't stop ringing! I decide to leave the door open so the guests can enter on their own. Entering into the kitchen with Mom and some of the guests, I help mix up Kyle's favorite punch. There's something about fruit punch, berries, sierra mist and rainbow sherbet that makes him act like he's five years old again.

Mom and I are stirring the punch when I hear the damn doorbell ring, again. "What. The. Hell," I mumble, aggravated. I stomp towards the foyer to open the door when Mom pulls me back by my elbow "I counted the guests earlier, and everyone that had an invitation is here," she states happily. Her eyes shine brightly, and she stares at me like I should know why she's giddy.

The doorbell sounds again and suddenly it hits me, "Oh my God! Mom! It's Kyle!" I scream excitedly, grabbing her hand, bouncing up and down.

She grips my hand and we sprint towards the door, eagerly opening it, ready to jump into Kyle's massive arms. But as our eyes come in contact with unfamiliar faces, we immediately freeze. Oh. My. Damn. It isn't Kyle greeting us. Instead, there are two men in uniform, and one of them is holding what appears to be a neatly folded American Flag. Now, I'm no expert at this military shit, but I'm pretty sure they aren't here to join the party.

I look over at my mom who is wide eyed and terrified. The soldier, who looks to be in his mid-thirties, steps forward and nods to my mother. "Are you Mrs. Lucille Anderson?" he asks.
All color drains from mom's face. She's speechless, and tears begin to pour down her cheeks. "Yes sir," she stammers, clutching her hands to her chest.

"Ma'am, we're her to inform you that your son, Sergeant Kyle Kayden Anderson of the..." his voice breaks as mom screams out in pain.

"No, no, no, no, no! It can't be," she repeats, gut wrenching sobs escaping her.
"Oh God...no," I mumble, realizing what their visit here entails.

The soldier continues on with his speech, but I can't focus. I can't comprehend, and I hear very few words coming from his mouth. The words I take in are "killed," "line of duty," "flag," "represents," and I immediately drop to my knees. I feel like I've been struck by lightning.

It takes work to keep breathing. I can't see; I can't hear, and I swear someone's reached through my chest and removed my heart. I see what's happening, but it can't be true...can it? My mother's on her knees, elbows on the floor, head hanging, and her body is violently shaking. The soldier is crouched down trying to comfort her, but she's pushing him away. I'm completely paralyzed and useless to her. This is a joke, right? Kyle is punking me. He has to be; he promised...

The cold water snaps me back into reality. I immediately cut the water off and step out onto the rug to dry myself. Going over to the vanity, I brush my teeth and hair, preparing myself for the day.

8

I take one last look in the mirror. “You'll survive.” If I can convince my brain that I'll be okay, maybe my heart will believe it too. I throw on some loose grey sweatpants with a white tank top and head downstairs to brew some coffee. No matter what's going on in my life, coffee makes it all better, for a few moments anyway.

As I step off the last stair that leads into the foyer, I stop dead in my tracks. The delicious roasted aroma overtakes my senses; it smells divine. After soaking up the coffee's delicious scent, I make my way through the living room to join my mother in the kitchen. For someone who buried her son yesterday, she doesn't look too bad. I mean, you can tell she's been crying by her red swollen eyes, but somehow, she has a peaceful look on her face. She's sitting at the island in the middle of our kitchen with a cup of coffee, reading her Bible.
“Morning love. Sleep well?” she asks, smiling up at me from under her lashes.

“No,” I admit, bemused. How can she be so calm after experiencing something so tragic? My soul is empty and a major piece of my heart's missing, and there's no way I could force a smile across my face. So, why isn't she mourning the loss of her one and only son?

“Figures. You look like crap,” she puckers.

“Way to brighten up my day,” I smirk.

She reaches over and pulls out the stool next to her. “Allie, come sit. There's something I want you to read.”

Walking to the counter across from the island, I pour myself a hot cup of black coffee. As the mug approaches my lips, I feel the heat from the steam; it's hot enough that it'll burn the hair off my tongue; however, it doesn't stop me from sipping it.

I enjoy the blissful feeling as the heat travels down my throat. Gently placing my coffee onto the counter, I slide into the stool beside her. “What ya got?” I hope she isn't going to shove her Bible down my throat. I was raised in a Christian home. I believe in God and all, but as you can imagine, I'm having a little difficulty in the faith department.

I'm not questioning God's existence. I just question his works. Our parents taught us that when two or more people gather in His name and agree on something, it'll happen, but what happened with my father? We laid hands on him and believed in his healing, but cancer took his life. Mom and I held hands each night and prayed for Kyle, and now, he's dead. So, I'm sure you can imagine my lack of faith.

Aw hell, here it comes “I came across this verse and I think it'd do you some good to read over it,” she insists, sliding her Bible in front of me.

“Mom, I really don't feel like reading that bullsh-,”

“Allie, don't finish that sentence!” she demands, cutting me off. “This isn't like you. Where's this attitude coming from, huh?”

“I haven't slept....my soul's been shattered, and the last man to ever love me is dead. That's where this is coming from! What I want to know is how you can sit here reading that shit, acting like everything's fine,” I yell at the top of my lungs.

She slams her coffee mug to the counter and scoots her stool away from the island. “Okay, I'm going to let that slide because I know you're hurting, but if you ever talk to me like that again, and most importantly, if you ever call God's word “shit” again, I'll knock every tooth in your mouth loose. You got that?” She turns away and storms out of the kitchen leaving her Bible wide open in front of me, exposing the highlighted verses.

With a roll of my eyes and an exhale of breath, I take a sip of coffee and relax. As I look down at the yellow highlighted lines, they draw my attention. Ecclesiastes, chapter 3 reads, “A time to be born and a time to die. A time to kill and a time to heal. A time to cry and a time to laugh. A time to grieve and a time to dance. A time to keep and a time to throw away. A time to tear and a time to mend. A time to love and a time to hate. A time for war and a time for peace."

Ironic, isn't it. It's the story of my life. My eyes begin to shed unwanted tears and a lump forms in my throat. If there's a time to heal, why isn't it happening to me, huh? Why are my wounds ripped open before they're able to scar? Hanging my head, I let the tears flow freely.

Mom sneaks behind me, gently laying her hand upon my shoulder. "Let it out, love. You'll feel better. It's okay to miss him, but you can't be angry at Kyle or with God. We'll all go through trials and tribulations, but you've got to stay strong in faith and depend on Him to get us through this devastating time. God's in control. Remember that, Al," she whispers.
Arguing with her is pointless, so I nod in agreement to avoid confrontation.